DISNEY
CHiLLS

ONCE UPON A SCREAM

by

Vera Strange

DISNEY PRESS

Los Angeles · New York

Copyright © 2022 Disney Enterprises, Inc.
Illustrations by Jeffrey Thomas

Printed in the United States of America
First Paperback Edition, August 2022
1 3 5 7 9 10 8 6 4 2
FAC-029261-22168
This book is set in Agmena Pro/Linotype
Designed by Megan Youngquist

Library of Congress Control Number: 2021952464
ISBN 978-1-368-07591-6

For more Disney Press fun, visit www.DisneyBooks.com

SUSTAINABLE
FORESTRY
INITIATIVE
Certified Chain of Custody
Promoting Sustainable Forestry
www.sfiprogram.org
SFI-01054
The SFI label applies to the text stock

The dreams that you FEAR will come true.

1
ONCE UPON A SCREAM

"**N**o . . . get off me!"

Once upon a scream, Dawn woke in a panic. She struggled in her bed, trying to tear off the roses pricking her skin and strangling her.

"Please, let me go!"

She sat upright and gasped for air. She glanced down, but the only thing wrapped around her body was the rosebud printed quilt.

No roses were choking her with their perfume. No thorns were stabbing her flesh. And no vines were wrapped around her body, dragging her down into the dirt and threatening to bury her alive.

It was all a terrible nightmare.

Even so, it took Dawn a moment to fully wake up. Remnants of deep sleep kept her brain in a spell.

The nightmare was so vivid that it held her in its terrifying grip. But there was more to it. Dawn rubbed her tired eyes, taking in her surroundings. Morning sunlight slanted through the white shutters, hitting the quilt on the bed in a crisscross pattern, reminding her of a jail cell.

Antique furniture took up the rest of the space, including an old wooden writing desk with a hutch, a stiff velvet-backed chair, an old-fashioned wardrobe with mirrored doors, and a canopy bed draped with yellowing lace that might have once been white. But Dawn couldn't be sure.

She blinked in confusion at the unfamiliar surroundings as she fully awakened, still feeling adrenaline making her heart pound. It took her a moment to remember where she was. Then, she frowned as her memories tumbled back.

Dawn wasn't in the big city anymore.

She was in the country, living with her two aunts. In fact, she had been in Castletown for three days already. And they felt like the longest days of her life. That was why she kept having this same nightmare every night.

Her parents had sent her away as a punishment.

The *incident* surfaced in her mind, even though she usually tried to forget it. Back home, Dawn had got caught shoplifting from the corner store with her two best friends.

Well, technically speaking . . . Dawn hadn't stolen anything.

But she was there when Ronnie palmed a lipstick, and Daniella stuffed the nail polish into her purse. And Dawn didn't try to stop them either, even though her heart was racing and she knew that it was wrong. They'd done a few things to break the rules before, like skipping class and sneaking off campus to get ice cream. But this was different.

They were breaking *real* laws this time.

The security guard busted them on the way out and called their parents. Even though Dawn argued that she didn't technically shoplift anything, her parents saw it differently. And the store security footage looked pretty bad, Dawn had to admit.

"But being there makes you an *accessory* to a crime," her mother said. She was a junkie for those procedural cop shows on late-night cable.

"Those girls are big trouble," her father added. "I always knew it. I tried to warn you, but you wouldn't listen to us. You said we were being *overprotective* and *controlling*."

Dawn cringed inside. Yup, those had been her exact words.

"Dawn Rosa Flores, what am I going to do with you?" her mom added in a histrionic voice. "You're not even a real teenager yet and already causing big problems."

Her mother only used her full name when she was really upset. That's how Dawn knew that this was a big deal and wouldn't blow over easily.

But still, she figured they'd ground her for a week or two. Maybe even a month. Take away her phone and computer privileges. Make her do some extra chores. The usual punishments they doled out whenever she bent . . . *broke* the rules.

But their solution shocked her. Dawn's parents

informed her that they'd spoken to her two aunts—Fleur and Merry—and they had agreed to take her into their home out in the country for the remainder of the school year. That meant *six whole months*.

Dawn felt a jolt of shock, chased by fiery anger.

"How can you do this to me?" she'd cried out. "This is so unfair!"

It wasn't that she didn't like her aunts. On the contrary, they were nice enough and always found a way to make her smile, even if they were a bit on the quirky side and spoke with thick Southern drawls. Aunt Fleur was her father's older sister, and she was married to Aunt Merry. Dawn hadn't seen them in person in a few years, since they lived so far away.

They lived in Castletown, which was located in the Deep South and didn't even have an airport, making a quick weekend trip there all but impossible. But she chatted with them on FaceTime just about every week, when they were catching up with her parents.

"How can you send your *child* away? It must be illegal or something. You can't just abandon me!" Dawn said, continuing her freak-out.

"Calm down and stop exaggerating," her father said in a stern voice. "We're not *abandoning* you."

"Aunts Fleur and Merry will take great care of you," her mother said reassuringly. "They love you, too."

"But I can't live in the middle of *freaking* nowhere!" Dawn continued, as the horror of her situation started to sink in. "What about my friends? What about my school?"

"Well, that's part of why we're doing it," her father replied in a measured voice. Angry tears tumbled down Dawn's cheeks.

Why didn't they understand how she felt?

Her parents explained that they wanted to get Dawn away from the "bad elements" in the city. The bad elements being her two best friends. But also, they argued, the crime rates were rising in their neighborhood and the public schools in their area also weren't that great.

Her parents couldn't relocate right now due to their jobs. Her mother was an ER nurse, while her father worked construction. Besides, they explained that this was only a "temporary solution" to get Dawn through the rest of the school year.

Dawn cried and raged and argued, then sulked before finally giving in. Not that she'd had a choice. She was being sent away.

And that was final.

Now, here she was . . . facing the rest of the school year in this backwards, middle-of-nowhere place named Castletown. The complete injustice of her situation dawned on her. In fact, now that she thought about it, everything about this place bugged her.

Literally.

For starters, it was too wild: there were so many icky insects, especially mosquitos that swarmed at sunset; also nature—stuff like trees, forests, snakes . . . and worst of all . . . poison ivy *and* poison oak.

Everything wanted to bite her, or poke her, or made her itch and sneeze. Or all of the above. Dawn was allergic to this place. She missed the concrete jungle of the city, dotted with parks, where nature was tamed and pruned into submission.

And the sun was too bright out in the country. Dawn was used to smog and towering buildings filtering out the daylight, casting the city in shadow. She also missed the adrenaline-fueled rush of navigating the city streets, dodging taxis and pedestrians and hopping on the crowded subway. She even missed the sirens and traffic noise, which blared all through the night. Out in the country, it was so quiet that it made it hard to fall asleep. She never knew that silence could actually keep you awake at night.

Castletown didn't even have a proper shopping mall or movie theater or any sort of public transportation. Her aunts lived way up a long, twisty dirt road with nary a neighbor in sight, unless you counted the chickens in the coop down by the rose garden. They were friendly enough but couldn't exactly hold a conversation.

In short, Dawn hated it here.

And most of all, she missed her two best friends. They were hundreds of miles away from Castletown, and even trying to text them was next to impossible.

She couldn't get a cell signal at their house, and the Wi-Fi was spotty, going in and out, making Dawn feel even more isolated. Occasionally, she could catch a signal on her phone if she crawled into the corner of her room and raised her hand as high as she could reach.

That's how she'd spent her first few days in Castletown, desperately searching for a signal so she could text-complain to Ronnie and Daniella . . . or watch the latest vids and social media posts. Her arms and shoulders would start to ache from holding the phone in such unnatural positions.

But mostly the vids froze halfway through loading or, worse, crashed her phone apps altogether, prompting her to throw her head back in defeat and grumble another round of "Argh I hate stupid Castletown!"

In addition, there was the endless list of chores that her aunts thrust on her—weeding out the rose garden, which triggered her allergies and stabbed her with their razor-sharp thorns; cleaning the chicken coop (major barf); hauling out the compost (extra-major barf), something so gross that she couldn't bear to ask what it actually was—or any other manual labor they could dream up for her.

With that morbid thought, Dawn forced herself out of bed, wincing at the chill in the air and the cold sting of the floorboards. She shivered in her thin pink nightgown. Her new bedroom always felt cold and drafty, even on a sunny day like this day was shaping up to be. The ancient radiators didn't heat the space evenly, or at all.

She quickly checked her phone, then frowned. No new messages. It was possible her friends hadn't texted her yet. It was pretty early in the morning. But a worse thought pinged her.

Did they forget about me?

More likely, the Wi-Fi was acting up, she forced herself to believe. Dawn stood up on her tiptoes and reached her arm into the corner, trying to catch a signal. She held that uncomfortable position for another long minute, until she started to cramp badly.

But still . . . no new messages appeared.

With a deep sigh, Dawn gave up and approached the wardrobe, taking in her reflection in the warped mirror. She had long black hair, from her mother, and bright green eyes, from her father. Her cheeks were high with a smattering of light brown freckles. Her eyes were puffy and her nose itched.

"Why am I allergic to . . . *Castletown*?" she said with a sharp sneeze. She shot an accusing glance at the window. Outside, she glimpsed a flash of dark red, almost like blood.

It was her aunts' rose garden maze, of course. But suddenly her horrible nightmare flashed through her head again. She remembered the roses stabbing and choking her.

Not only was the rose garden probably the catalyst for her bad dream, but it was also the instigator of her daily sneezing fits. Of all things, it turned out that Dawn was terribly allergic to roses, and lucky for her, Castletown happened to be the "Rose Capital of the South."

The town slogan was even "Stop to Smell the Roses," as the cheerful hand-carved sign had informed her when her aunts drove her through the tiny downtown for the first time. Every shop and store, and even the planters alongside the road, sported bushels of roses stretching their delicate petals toward the sun, making the town an eccentric roadside tourist attraction, vital to the local businesses.

Her aunts' two-story stone cottage was situated on a large parcel of land that spanned seven acres, all the way up to the dark forest that surrounded their quaint farm, allowing them to indulge in their great passion for gardening, which was second only to their passion for collecting and selling antiques at their shop, called Spindles 'N' Things.

In fact, while the farm's chickens were the source of eggs, more importantly, their droppings made for the best fertilizer to grow roses, her aunts had kindly informed her on her first day, not realizing how much that idea made Dawn want to puke.

Dawn, after reflecting on all this, returned her gaze to the window. The rosebushes themselves were shaped into neat hedges that wound into an intricate maze, which apparently became a sort of tourist attraction in the summer season that allowed her aunts some extra money and stirred up business for their antique shop.

Nothing fun or interesting ever happened in Castletown, Dawn felt. Proving her point was the fact that a bunch of dumb flowers that made her sneeze were the place's main draw.

The rose maze took up the whole backyard. It was also super easy to get lost in. Dawn knew because she'd spent her first day there lost inside the maze, trying to find her way out, until her aunts took pity and fetched her for dinner.

"You can't trust roses," she remembered Aunt Merry telling her as they led her out of the labyrinth. She glanced at the wrought iron sign: ROSE GARDEN MAZE—ENTER IF YOU DARE!

"Oh, and why's that?" Dawn asked, stifling another sneeze.

"Because they trick you, dearie," Aunt Merry chirped. She always managed to sound like a tiny cheerful bluebird. And in her old-fashioned periwinkle dresses (blue was the only color she'd wear), she looked like one, too. But her comment sounded menacing. It made Dawn shiver.

"Trick you . . . how so?" Dawn asked, arching her eyebrow. She then shot a glance back at the maze. She wouldn't venture back there anytime soon.

"You see, roses lure you in to smell them with their beauty and perfume," Aunt Fleur replied, fluttering around like a slightly larger cardinal. Unlike Aunt Merry, she always wore red dresses. "Only to prick you."

Merry touched a thorn, then grimaced as she held

up her index finger. A small drop of blood stained her pale skin.

"Oh, no! Let's get you patched up," Aunt Fleur said. "Hold on, I'll mix up some healing salve. We'll have you fixed up in a jiffy."

But Dawn just stared at the dark red dollop of blood on the pad of Aunt Merry's finger, while Fleur worked to gather strong-smelling herbs from the garden to make the remedy. Dawn didn't know what a *salve* was, only that everything in Castletown felt different and strange.

Ding!

Her phone chimed mercifully with an incoming text message pushing the memory out of her mind. The Wi-Fi signal was working again. She dove for the bedside table and swiped it up, clutching eagerly for any last tether to her old city life. She felt relief as she saw her two best friends' names—*Ronnie* and *Daniella*—pop up on the screen. She scanned the messages in their group chat, her heart racing.

RONNIE: *Hey, little country mouse! How's it going in the wilderness?*

DANIELLA: *Seriously, us city girls misssssssssssssss you!*

Dawn typed back to them, her fingers flying over the keyboard.

DAWN: *Awww, I thought you forgot about me . . .* 😔

Dots appeared as they typed their replies. Dawn held her breath and prayed that the signal didn't pull a vanishing act again. Finally, their messages flashed onto the chat. Dawn scanned them, soaking up this last connection to her old life.

RONNIE: *Ugh, not a chance! Our parents took our phones away. They are the worst.*

DANIELLA: *Yeah, we just got them back . . . finally!* ♡

RONNIE: *You're our first text. BFF . . . we'd never forget you, gurl.*

They texted a selfie of them on the subway, riding it to school. It took forever to come through. Finally, the picture loaded onto the screen. Ronnie was short and vivacious, with curly dark hair, wide lips, and light brown skin, while Daniella was dark-skinned with long frosted hair and sharp eyes. They both made goofy faces. It was captioned *Miss you!*

Dawn gazed at the selfie, feeling her heart ache fiercely like a bruise in her chest. Ronnie and Daniella lived in the same apartment building across the street from Dawn's family. They'd all become fast friends as little kids, playing hopscotch with pastel chalk scratched on the city sidewalks, dodging pedestrians and dogs and skipping and hopping together, eventually graduating to the same kindergarten and now middle school. . . .

Together.

If there was one word to describe their friendship, that was it. The three of them did everything *together*—even getting into trouble, as it turned out.

But now Dawn was stuck here alone, in the middle of nowhere, a punishment almost worse than death for a thirteen-year-old city girl whose friends were having fun back home without her.

It's just so not fair, Dawn thought again for the thousandth—*no, millionth*—time. The "if only" constantly swam through her head. *If only* . . . they hadn't gotten caught. *If only* . . . Dawn had done a better job distracting the clerk or spotted the security guard. *If only* . . . Ronnie and Daniella had moved quicker. But none of that mattered now.

They did get caught. And Dawn got sent away. That couldn't be changed.

With a sigh, Dawn typed back with a selfie of her own, lying on her bed with an exaggerated frown, but the signal was again too weak, and it bounced right back.

DAWN: *Ugh, it's so dumb here! Plus, the wifi is terrible. There's nothing to do. Everything is far away. I hate Castletown.* ☹

Her friends wrote back quickly, trying their best to cheer her up. Their upbeat messages crowded her screen, making Dawn feel less alone than she had in three long days.

DANIELLA: *Hang in there, gurl! The school year will be over in a flash.*

RONNIE: *And we'll have a big party to celebrate when you get back.*

Dawn read and reread their messages, feeling her spirits lift. Her friends were the best. They hadn't forgotten about her, and as soon as Dawn got back, they'd be thick as thieves again.

Well . . . thick as *reformed* thieves. Dawn was done with breaking laws and getting into trouble. She'd learned her lesson big-time.

RONNIE: *It's so not fair they sent you away. We only got grounded for two weeks.*

DANIELLA: *For real, it's like we've been living in the Dark Ages.*

DAWN: *I'd take the Dark Ages over . . . Castletown.* 😃

Why had Dawn's parents overreacted this way?

Ronnie was right—it wasn't fair.

With a defeated sigh, Dawn pulled up her phone and texted her friends a frown/tear emoji and started to write a reply, when suddenly—

Her aunts' high-pitched voices echoed through the rickety cottage and up the stairs to her bedroom.

"Wake up, Sleeping Beauty!" Fleur chirped at her; then Merry added to the chorus. "You're going to be late for your first day at school!"

2
FLEUR AND MERRY

"**D**on't make us come up there and fetch you!" Aunt Fleur called.

Dawn grimaced at the irritating chirp of their voices. It cut through the house like a birdsong—the kind that wakes you at the crack of dawn.

"Coming!" Dawn called back, forcing the annoyance from her voice.

It was her first day of sixth grade at her new school, and she was already dreading it. Back home, she'd loved her old public school for one reason: her friends were there.

Ronnie and Daniella were the reason she had bounced out of bed every day, excited to meet up at the station right outside their apartment buildings.

What was more terrifying than starting over at a brand-new school? Where you didn't know anybody? In a brand-new town?

And worse, it was . . .

Middle school.

That made her even more nervous. Dawn had no idea what to expect. Her aunts had registered her before she arrived in town, so she hadn't visited Castletown Middle School yet.

But she had to go to school, of course, and she had to be on time. She couldn't afford to be marked tardy. This was her last chance to prove to her parents that she wasn't "trouble" and "causing problems" anymore, so that she could go back home.

You can do this, she promised herself, as she dragged her tired body out of bed and opened the wardrobe. The doors made the worst screeching noise. *Creaaaakkkkkkk.*

She plugged her ears and shuddered in annoyance. If her aunts' high-pitched voices hadn't already jerked her fully awake, the wardrobe made sure of it.

No more sleeping beauty, she thought, as she selected her outfit, pulling it out of the drawers, which smelled like mildew and mothballs. She slid into her clothes, then shut the wardrobe, releasing another earsplitting creak, and glanced in the mirrors on the doors.

Her warped reflection stared back at her. She wore a tight ribbed pink top and ripped jeans, the fashionable kind. But now she felt unsure. Dawn looked down at herself. She felt insecurity rush through her. Just like her old life, suddenly her old clothes felt all wrong here.

Would she fit in? Would the other kids like her?

Uncertainty stabbed her like a rose's thorns. But she wasn't about to borrow a frumpy old dress from her aunts, right?

She shuddered at the thought of showing up to her first day at her new school in one of their ugly blue or red fashion monstrosities. Their dresses were probably secondhand, too, like everything else.

Anyway, she was already running late. She didn't have time to change.

Dawn snapped a quick mirror selfie, found that one spot in the corner where she could snag a weak Wi-Fi signal, and shot a text to her friends, asking how she looked in her outfit and promising to FaceTime them right after school.

But it took forever for the transmission to go through. "Come on," Dawn begged her phone, watching the text struggle to send. "Please, I need this. . . . Just send already!" Finally, her phone chimed.

She waited, dots flashed . . . then her friends' replies flooded the screen.

RONNIE: *You look so rad. Show them country mice how it's done!*

DANIELLA: *Oh, love the pink top! Good luck today. Make loads of new friends.*

RONNIE: *But not too many! Don't forget ur city girls!*

That made Dawn smile in spite of herself. Her mood instantly improved. She texted them back a slew of pink heart emojis that filled the whole screen. She could *never* replace them.

They were her best friends, and they always would be . . . period.

In fact, her whole plan was to be on her best behavior

so she could get back home as soon as possible. Nothing was going to stop her. But then, another thought occurred to her: she needed to make new friends ASAP. Plus, she decided as she hatched her new plan, if she made friends with "nice" kids—in short, the kind her parents would approve of, the kind who would never, ever shoplift— maybe she could convince her mom and dad that she had changed her ways and could go home earlier.

With that hopeful thought, Dawn snagged her backpack and made her way down the creaky staircase, hoping that she didn't get a splinter from the worn floorboards.

When she reached the living room, she glanced through the window on the front door. The sun had risen a little more and drenched the outside surroundings in golden light.

Beyond their stone cottage lay a thick forest that stretched up to the foothills of a forbidding-looking mountain range. It towered over everything in town with its sharp, snow-covered peaks poking at the sky and crowned by rings of misty clouds.

The view reminded Dawn of something out of an old fairy tale, something ancient and filled with dangerous magic. Most people would have called it beautiful or charming even, but it only made Dawn feel sad. She didn't know you could miss buildings, but she did.

Dawn dragged her gaze away from the mountains, then hurried into the kitchen, which smelled of eggs and bacon and something else . . . something sweet, perfumy, and—

"Achoo!"

She sneezed violently. Through the open windows, the rose garden maze released its sickly-sweet aroma, which wafted inside the cottage, triggering Dawn's allergies.

"Oh, my heavens," Aunt Fleur said in alarm, stepping back from the wood-fired stove. She wore an old-fashioned red dress, as always, with a red cape. Her gray hair was tucked into a top bun.

"Dearie, how about a spot of tea?" Aunt Merry added, putting an old teakettle to boil on the cast-iron burner. "It'll clear you right up."

Aunt Merry was shorter and younger than Fleur. She wore a blue dress and cape. Unlike her wife's, Merry's hair was jet-black but pulled back in the same style. She even had on a blue cap that matched her dress.

They talked with slow thick Southern drawls that made it hard for Dawn to understand sometimes, unlike back in the city, where everyone spoke a million miles a minute, like they were in a rush to get somewhere; probably because they were.

"Uh, thanks," Dawn said, stifling a sniffle. "That sounds great."

She took a seat at the kitchen table, while her aunts bustled around making tea and cooking eggs and bacon, sizzling in fat she'd learned was called lard. The kitchen was terribly old-fashioned, like everything else in the house. There wasn't even a microwave or a coffeemaker in sight. The freezer was separate from the fridge. It was the kind that opened like a treasure chest.

None of the furniture matched, either. The worn wooden kitchen table sported six different sorts of chairs, all with various colored seat cushions.

Dawn guessed that most of this junk came from their antique shop. She missed her old apartment and its modern furniture. It might have been made of flimsy particleboard and purchased from IKEA, but at least it was new and didn't smell funny. Her parents had assembled it all, struggling with the instructions, which looked more like some kind of super-difficult math test.

"Oh, dearie, here you go," Merry said, pouring piping hot liquid from a chipped porcelain teapot painted with roses and dragons into an equally battered teacup. She set it on a saucer in front of Dawn, who eyed the steaming liquid with great suspicion.

The tea looked brown and murky, and it smelled strong and medicinal. A few leaves were floating in it, too. But she forced herself to take one sip, then almost spit it out.

"Wh-what is it?" she coughed.

It tasted . . . awful, like cough syrup.

"Oh, silly, Merry makes it from the herbs in the garden," Aunt Fleur chimed in from the kitchen. "Pluck up and drink it! It's good for ya."

Dawn's eyes flicked to Aunt Fleur and Aunt Merry, who were busily stoking the fire in the stove and mixing up strange, almost witchy concoctions from herbs and plants from their garden.

Suddenly, out of nowhere, a rush of homesickness hit Dawn so hard that it felt like the wind was knocked out of her. In that moment—in this strange kitchen, in this weird place—she missed her parents terribly.

They drank rich, dark coffee spiked with thick cream and brown sugar, not disgusting, bitter tea. And they made it in a shiny new coffeemaker that burbled. In fact, they were probably sitting in the kitchen right now, doing just that . . .

Without her.

Anger and love simmered in her heart simultaneously. She missed her parents like crazy, but they were also the ones who had sent her to the middle of nowhere. It was a confusing mixture of emotions. Kind of like a rose, which was both beautiful and dangerous, as her aunt had explained, with sharp thorns lurking just underneath the delicate petals and sweet perfume.

Dawn pushed the tea away; her appetite had vanished. Her stomach churned unhappily with the bitter liquid she had swallowed. This was just one more thing in a long list of things that bothered her.

Oh, Mama and Papa . . . I miss you, Dawn thought.

Her aunts' voices snapped her out of her thoughts.

"Oh, look at the time!" Merry chirped in alarm,

gesturing to the antique clock ticking away above the sink. "We've got to hurry!"

"Goodness gracious, you're gonna be late for school," Fleur added with a flutter. They hustled Dawn to the door.

How mortifying, Dawn thought as she slung her backpack over her shoulders and clomped toward the lonely-looking mailbox at the end of the drive, where she had to wait for the bus.

Back in the city, riding the school bus was decidedly . . . *uncool.* Oblivious to her torment, her aunts called cheerfully to her.

"See you after school!" Merry chirped, waving from the front door. "We'll pick you up to take you to the shop. We've got a bunch of chores waiting for you."

"We had to let our sales assistant go last month," Fleur chimed in. "So, we really need your help. You're gonna be a lifesaver."

They peered at their niece expectantly. Their arms fluttered about, almost like fairy wings.

As if this day could get any worse, Dawn thought in frustration.

She pictured the quaint storefront in the center of town with the golden awning that read Spindles 'N' Things.

If you asked Dawn, the antique shop was dusty, gross, and filled with a bunch of smelly old junk that made her crinkle her nose in disgust. She didn't understand why anyone would want any of that broken, used stuff when they could shop for brand-new furniture.

But when she complained about it to her parents, they argued that working for her aunts would teach her "responsibility" and "work ethic," whatever that meant. Also, it turned out this was part of the deal that they'd made with her aunts for taking her into their home. For the past year, their shop had been struggling to stay afloat.

Dawn forced a smile, even though this was the last way she wanted to spend her afternoon. She wanted to text or FaceTime her friends, or simply sulk in her bedroom. But she had to be on her best behavior if she wanted her exile to end quickly.

"Of course, can't wait!" Dawn mumbled through stiff, pressed lips. "See you after school."

"Have a good day!" her aunts called as the yellow bus roared down the gravel road, coughing out black exhaust.

But Dawn knew the truth.

Unless they could do magic and miraculously teleport her back to the city . . . and her friends . . . and her parents . . . and her school . . . and her old life, then there was no way this was going to be a good day.

Ugh, make it end already.

3
HAIL TO THE PRINCESS

Vrooooooom! Hiss!

The bus spit Dawn out at the entrance to Castletown Middle School. As the other kids streamed off into the quaint redbrick school building, chattering away and messing with each other, she found herself standing alone.

Dawn had one thought.

This school is so ... small.

It was just one building, whereas her old school had several connected by paths marred by chewing gum and what was supposed to be grass but was really just trampled patches of mud.

You can do this, she told herself, remembering what her friends had texted.

The time would pass quickly. Plus, she could make new friends—the "nice" kind—in the meantime, right? Also, her friends had reassured her how cute her outfit was: this was the latest fashion, she felt confident.

Buoyed by those thoughts, Dawn took a deep breath, smoothed out her jeans, and re-tucked her tank top in—then plunged into the building. The familiar school aroma hit her nostrils, pungent, since kids were packing the hallways. Despite it being a small building, inside it looked and smelled like any other middle school—like rubber bands and bleach and bubble gum, making her feel more comfortable.

She checked her schedule, then headed for the classroom down the hall for sixth graders. Her old school had several sections of sixth grade classes, each with well over thirty kids. But her new school had only one section for each grade. She braced herself and poked her head through the door.

Warily, Dawn scanned the space. She was the first kid

to arrive. However, based on the way desks were evenly spaced around the room, it looked like there would be about twenty kids in the class, tops.

But other than the smaller size, it resembled any other classroom. Whiteboard, teacher's desk, overly cheerful posters, rows of student desks.

But something else surprised her.

This classroom sported modern technology, with banks of brand-new computers lined up against the wall. They were much nicer than the ones in her old city school. Dawn could see modern lab equipment tucked away in the glass cupboards along the walls.

Likewise, the kids wandering in clutched the latest phones and vid game consoles, much fancier than her used phone handed down from her parents.

Dawn had expected these kids to be behind the times, but she now realized that was a flawed assumption. Actually, she was the one who was behind the times.

Feeling self-conscious, she slipped her phone into her pocket, lest anyone notice and decide it was a reason to shun her. She badly wanted to make friends that day.

You can do this, she told herself again.

"Hey, you the new kid?"

The question shot across the room unexpectedly, hitting Dawn and making her jump.

They were already calling her that.

But she took a deep breath and steeled herself, then turned around in a casual way. Or at least, she hoped it appeared casual. In reality, her heart was thumping out of control and her palms were sweating like crazy.

She forced a smile.

Her eyes landed on a cluster of three girls standing in the doorway. They were dressed prim and formally in nice, matching pastel dresses and Mary Jane shoes, like they were headed for Sunday church services.

Even the boys were dressed nicely in khakis or slacks, paired with button-down or polo shirts in a variety of pastel colors.

Dawn looked down at herself, taking in her ripped jeans and tight tank. She felt a jolt of insecurity rush through her. In fact, now that she saw the other kids filing in and taking their seats, she realized how badly she stuck out.

She wished she could change her outfit, but she didn't have a choice. She had to face her fate.

She flashed the three girls a charming smile.

"Right, I answer to many names," Dawn said, trying to be both chill and funny, a tricky combination, but one that she hoped she'd mastered. "*New* kid. *Cool* kid. *Smart* kid."

A moment of awkward silence passed.

The girls just stared at her like she was a new exhibit in a zoo.

"But since we're gonna be friends," Dawn added as she forced herself to continue anyway, sticking out her hand in greeting, projecting confidence, "you can just call me Dawn. Like the morning."

Still, the girls said nothing. They just stared at her. Dawn started to worry. Okay, not just worry, but downright panic. Her heart raced.

But then one of the girls—the one in the light blue dress—cracked a smile and sauntered toward her. The others followed suit, as if the first girl was pulling their strings.

"Nice to meet you, Dawn," she said with a shy smile. "I'm Leah. Welcome to Castletown."

Leah had sunshine-gold hair and lips red as the town's

renowned roses. She reminded Dawn of a fairy-tale princess, and she acted the part perfectly. She didn't just walk. It was like she floated.

"That's Kaylee," Leah went on, nudging the dark-haired girl to her right. "And this gal here is Stephanie," she added, nudging the other girl, with curly red hair and cinnamon eyes.

They tittered shyly, so Leah nudged them again and shot them a pouty look. "Well, now, don't forget your Southern charm," Leah drawled in a sugary-sweet voice. "Say hi, girls."

"*Hi, girls,*" Kaylee said, smirking as she imitated Leah's voice and cadence perfectly.

"Pleased to meet you, Dawn like the morning," Stephanie added.

They all spoke with accents, Dawn observed, like her aunts. These girls sounded more formal than Dawn's old friends. She couldn't tell if they were being nice or if they were making fun of her.

Or maybe a little bit of both.

"Uh . . . hi back," Dawn said, in an attempt to sound more like them.

"Just so you know, Leah's the princess of Castletown," Kaylee whispered, leaning in.

"Hail to the princess," added Stephanie with a curtsy. "You're meeting Southern royalty."

"What do you mean?" Dawn asked.

"Oh, you really are new here!" Kaylee said. "I thought everyone knew. Leah's father is the mayor of Castletown. That's pretty much like being the king 'round these parts."

"Which makes her mom the queen," Stephanie added. "So that makes Leah . . ."

"The princess of Castletown," Dawn finished for them, putting all the pieces together.

"Knock it off, y'all," Leah said, giggling. "Quit making me blush. Y'all are just buttering me up cuz it's my birthday party tomorrow."

"Well, it is *the* social event of sixth grade," Kaylee said. "Not every day our princess turns thirteen."

"Yup, it's gonna be the best party of the year," Stephanie added. "I'd simply die if I didn't get an invite."

"Oh, hush now," Leah chided them. But her eyes narrowed. "Of course, I'm inviting y'all. Who else is gonna be in my royal court?"

Dawn took this all in, trying to process how strange these girls sounded with their accents and to decipher the social dynamics of this new school. But one thing was very clear: she needed to score an invitation to Leah's birthday party if she wanted to make friends here to help her survive her exile without going crazy. Plus, these were clearly the nice, popular girls in Castletown.

"So, what's it take to land an invite to your party?" Dawn asked. "Sounds like I don't wanna miss it. Must be the social event of the season."

Leah exchanged looks with her friends, then twisted her lips into a charming smile. "Darlin', I'll let you know tomorrow," Leah said. "I've gotta check with my parents first."

With that, they floated away toward their desks, leaving Dawn standing by the classroom door.

A party! Dawn thought, feeling excited. At least, that sounded like something fun to do around this boring town. Maybe her luck was starting to turn around after all. She was glad she tried to talk to Leah even though she was nervous about being the "new kid."

"Students, take your seats," their teacher, Mr.

Blankenship, called from the front of the class. He swept his eyes over the room. "Don't make me mark y'all tardy."

He wore a short-sleeved white button-up shirt, red-striped tie, and thick black-rimmed glasses. Adding to the look, his close-cropped white hair gave him the appearance of an actor from an old Hollywood movie.

The other students hurried inside, jockeying for desks, while their teacher took his place in front of the whiteboard and shuffled papers. Dawn followed the rush. Only two desks remained unclaimed, all the way at the back of the class. Dawn headed for one.

Ring!

Suddenly, right at the bell, another girl burst into the room. She was clutching the biggest pile of library books Dawn had ever seen. She looked panicked and gestured around wildly, almost dropping her books.

"Sorry, Mr. Blankenship!" the girl exclaimed. "Samson wasn't feeling so good this morning. Uh, it was pretty icky. That's why I'm late—"

"Phillipa, spare me the sordid details," Mr. Blankenship said in a dry voice. Laughter echoed around the room.

But Dawn was just confused. Why were they laughing if someone in her family was sick?

"At least he didn't eat her homework this time!" a boy blurted out.

Phillipa blushed fiercely, as more giggles exploded from the class. *Someone in her family ate her homework?* Dawn pictured a feral little brother, or maybe a scary grandpa with dentures.

"Right, but he *really* did eat it," Phillipa protested, her face turning a deeper red, like an apple. "He's like always hungry. I'm lucky he hasn't tried to eat me, too."

More giggles roiled through the class, but Dawn was horrified. The girl's little brother was a cannibal? She'd once seen part of a horror movie about the South with that in it.

But then, the girl continued. "Probably cuz he's so big. He's a giant sheepdog."

Oh, Dawn realized. That made more sense. She found herself laughing, too. And also relaxing. These kids were like any other kids.

"Okay, enough!" Mr. Blankenship said. "Let's get

started. Phillipa, take your seat. We're starting with math today," he added, as loud groans of protest broke out around the room.

"Yes, sir," Phillipa said, hunching her shoulders. She slid into the desk next to Dawn and slumped over.

She plopped the books on her desk, making it shudder under the weight. Dawn glimpsed images of fairies, witches, wizards, dragons, and more on their whimsical illustrated covers.

Unlike Leah and her prim friends, Phillipa wore dusty overalls and muddy boots. Her hair was scraped back into a messy ponytail. Were those pieces of straw and leaves stuck in it, too?

Phillipa shot Dawn a look, giving her a good once-over. Then, like everyone else in the town, who spoke to strangers without an invitation, she whispered to Dawn.

"Hey there," Phillipa said. "You're the new girl? Your aunts told my pop about ya."

"Wait, does everyone in this town know everything?" Dawn asked, taken aback.

She made sure to keep her voice low and her eyes trained forward. Back home at her old school, she and her friends were practically experts at getting away with talking during class.

Phillipa nodded, while Mr. Blankenship scrawled math problems on the whiteboard.

"They surely do," Phillipa whispered back, keeping her eyes forward, too. Her accent sounded rougher, more country. "Folks 'round these parts talk to everybody. And they know everybody else's *darn* business, or so my pop says."

"Wow, the people here are so nice and friendly," Dawn whispered to Phillipa. "I'm used to the city, I guess."

"What's it like up there?" the girl asked with an excited grin. "I've never been outside Castletown. Unless you count hiking in the forest."

"Well, let's see . . . in the city . . . it's not like they're trying to be mean exactly," Dawn said, thinking it over. "More like everyone is always in a rush and too busy to stop and chat."

"Must be something," Phillipa whispered. "All those people. All those buildings and cars. I heard about the train that runs underground. I've never even seen a real subway, just on TV."

"Yeah, I miss it," Dawn said, feeling a pang of homesickness. But then she caught herself. She had to make it work here. That was her way of getting back home. "But friendly is good, too. Even Leah and her friends Stephanie and Kaylee were super nice."

Phillipa's face fell at the mention of Leah. Dawn noticed it. "Uh, what's wrong?"

"Right, just be careful of Leah and her friends," Phillipa said in a low voice.

Dawn frowned. "What's that mean?"

"They seem nice enough all right," Phillipa whispered. "But nice on the outside doesn't always mean nice on the inside. My pop told me that, too."

Dawn wanted to ask more questions, but then it was time for a math pop quiz.

She felt herself cringing at the prospect. When Mr. Blankenship passed it out, he stopped by her desk and set the paper down.

He shot her a kind smile, spotting the look of horror on her face.

"Not a math fan, huh?"

"Yeah, I guess not." Dawn swallowed hard. It had never been her best subject. And she had to get good grades and do well in school, or her parents would be angry and leave her in exile. For her, that was a fate worse than death.

"If it's okay, I'd like you to give the quiz a shot," Mr. Blankenship replied, tapping the paper. "But since you're new to class, the grade won't count. I'll give you a free pass this time."

"Really?" Dawn said, feeling like she'd just got a get-out-of-jail-free card in a game.

He smiled down at her. "Just do your best, okay? That's all I ask. And if you need extra help with math, we'll make sure you get it. I'm here to help you, not punish you."

Wow, that is so different. Dawn felt herself warming from the inside out. Back home, her teachers weren't quite as kind about math quizzes.

Of course, they had bigger classes and often seemed frustrated and stretched thin.

Maybe Castletown isn't so bad, Dawn decided. She was still dreading working at the antique shop after school and the litany of chores awaiting her in its dusty aisles. But with any luck, she'd get an invitation to Leah's birthday party the next day.

Thinking of the party, Dawn struggled to keep focused on the quiz. She loved parties of all kinds. They were always so fun. Finally, she'd have something to do besides getting lost in rose mazes.

Her eyes darted to Leah and her friends, sitting in the front row of the class in their matching dresses and shiny patent leather shoes.

Suddenly, Leah's hand shot up. "All finished, Mr. Blankenship!" she called out.

She was already done?

The rest of the class was still scribbling away. Phillipa had her tongue stuck out and was biting it in concentration. Dawn had barely answered three questions out of twenty, and they were probably all wrong. Fortunately, she had a free pass that day.

"I'd expect nothing less from my top student," Mr. Blankenship responded, as Leah handed in her quiz. "Guessing it's another A-plus?"

"Yes, sir," Leah said. "That would be the best birthday gift, wouldn't it?"

Mr. Blankenship gave her a pleased look. "Of course! I'm sure you aced it."

Wow, Leah really is like a princess around here, Dawn thought as she watched them. She was nice and smart, and—best of all—Leah was going to be Dawn's new best friend. Dawn would make sure of it. Maybe if they became friends, Leah could even help Dawn improve her math grades.

What could be better?

4
UNTIL PROVEN
GUILTY... NOT

Dawn burst into school the next day feeling excited. She was going to score an invite to Leah's birthday party and, better yet, solidify her new friendships. That was her ticket to surviving the rest of the school year in Castletown.

The day was already off to a great start. For the first time in a week, Dawn had slept well. She had been exhausted after going to school and working the whole afternoon at the antique shop. But she'd whistled the whole time. Even her aunts had noticed her change in attitude, smiling to themselves because their niece was adjusting well. Dawn hadn't even had a single nightmare.

She had fallen into a deep sleep and had woken up eager for school, too.

That morning, she'd bounced out of bed bright and early, found a weak signal in the corner, and texted Ronnie and Daniella, telling them about Leah and the birthday party.

DAWN: *Good news! I made my first friend here.* ☺ *And she's having a birthday party!*

DANIELLA: *Already? Wow . . . that was fast. Like really fast.*

RONNIE: *I doubt that stupid party will be as fun as our parties.*

DAWN: *Oh, not even close. But a party is a party. I'll take it. I need to make new friends if I'm gonna survive this parental-imposed exile.*

There was a long pause before they responded, and this time it wasn't due to a spotty signal. Dawn wondered if they were texting each other behind her back, away from the group chat they always used. After another excruciating long minute—way longer than it usually took them to respond—Dawn tried texting them again.

She worried she was reading far too much into it and overanalyzing the situation, but they were her best friends. She knew them all too well.

Her fingers flew over the keyboard before she could hold back and act more chill (something she wasn't great at anyway).

DAWN: *Aren't you happy for me? I can make friends here, right? Uh, do you want me to be alone with my weird aunts? For 6 whole months?* ☹

Another excruciating long pause followed. Dawn worried that she'd overstepped and was acting needy and dramatic (something her mother often accused her of— "teenage ways").

DANIELLA: *Okay, but don't forget about us.* 😉
RONNIE: *Yeah, we're still your best friends. Right?*
DAWN: *Always.* 😎😎😎

But there was more to it than that. Dawn had been looking forward to telling them about her first day at school and how she'd made new friends already. And especially, she couldn't wait to share the news about Leah's party.

Leah was clearly the most popular girl at school. Plus, based on how she and her friends Stephanie and Kaylee dressed for school, the party would probably be super fancy, Dawn figured. She couldn't wait to get her official invitation at school that day and find out. Her aunts would surely give her the afternoon off from work to get ready, seeing as they wanted her to make friends there.

Dawn had never been to a fancy party before. Just more "hangs" or casual birthdays back in the city. Her friends weren't elegant like Leah and the kids in Castletown.

While Ronnie and Daniella had sounded excited for Dawn, at least on the surface, she could tell that something was a little bit off about their reactions. Those weird pauses were unsettling.

They're jealous, she realized in surprise.

And afraid of losing her as a friend. But friendships could be hard and unpredictable sometimes. Besides, what choice did Dawn have? Did her old friends want her to spend the next six months alone, sulking in her bedroom? She needed to make new friends if she was going to survive. Period.

With that thought, she scanned the hall. She spotted Leah, along with her royal court of Kaylee and Stephanie, by their classroom. They were dressed in pastel dresses again, just like the day before. Leah waved Dawn over right away.

Dawn had come prepared. She'd fished out her one nice dress from the back of the wardrobe, the one her mom had insisted she bring in case her aunts decided to take her to church or some other gathering. Of course she'd argued with her mom about bringing it, unable to imagine why she'd need that out in the country. But now she was grateful.

The dress was black and purple, not pastel like what Leah and the girls in her entourage wore. But it was velvet and long, sweeping around her ankles with lace trim. She'd paired it with black dress shoes. They were a bit clunkier and made for the city and walking, unlike the girls' Mary Janes.

But she was dressed up for school for once, and she knew she'd fit in better. She even carried herself differently, walking with her shoulders back and head high. Dawn had also applied a bit of pink lip gloss, thrilled her aunts didn't react or, worse, forbid it.

Instead, when she trotted into the kitchen that morning, they'd oohed and aahed at her appearance. "Oh dearie, look at that dress!" Merry trilled. "It's beautiful."

"You look tremendous," Fleur piped up. "Just wonderful."

At school, Dawn made a beeline down the hall, trying to act nonchalant and not too eager, even though her heart was racing. They gave her "slow up and settle down" looks, though their faces said nothing.

Dawn knew the drill. She kept her face neutral.

"Happy b-day," Dawn said in her best casual-cool voice. She added a shrug for good measure to show she wasn't that eager. "Welcome to the official teen club."

Leah gave her a respectful nod. "Thirteen queens."

"You're already thirteen?" Kaylee asked Dawn, sounding envious.

"What's it like?" Stephanie added. "Me and Kaylee are still only twelve."

"Guess you'll have to wait and find out," Dawn

quipped back, loving the attention. She arched her eyebrow at Leah for extra effect, showing they were the cool ones here.

Leah shot her a conspiratorial smile, while Stephanie and Kaylee looked jealous.

"Come to think of it, I do feel more grown-up already," Leah said smugly, focusing on Dawn and leaning closer. "Of course, Ma says I've always been mature for my age."

"I can see that," Dawn said, projecting confidence. Then she made herself ask the question burning in her heart. "So, did you ask your parents if I could come to your party today?"

Leah exchanged looks with her friends, then reached into her bag and produced a pale pink envelope sealed with a rose sticker.

An invitation! Dawn thought in excitement, but then she made herself calm down. She didn't want to blow the whole thing.

"As promised," Leah said with a wink. "Here you go. Open it."

Dawn accepted the envelope, then peeled back the delicate sticker. Inside was rich cream-colored card stock. It had Leah's initials embossed on top. But it didn't say anything about a birthday party. Dawn was confused.

"Well, you gonna read it?" Leah said, giving her an expectant look.

Dawn unfolded the card, then felt horror rush through her like ice water. She read the card, praying that there was some mistake. Inside, one word was written in bold letters:

CRIMINAL

Dawn's face fell — or more like crumpled — in on itself. Tears tugged at her eyes, pricking them with shame. Meanwhile, Leah and her friends broke out in jeers and laughter.

"Look at her face!" Leah said through giggles. "She actually thought I'd invite her to *my* birthday party. As if!"

Dawn wheeled around, noticing that all the kids in the hall had stopped to stare at them. Then she heard it. . . .

"Criminal," the kids whispered, pointing to her and laughing. The word shot through the hall.

"How . . . do you know about that?" Dawn managed to spit out. The shoplifting incident flashed through her head like a bad dream.

Leah smirked at her. "Well, we did a little digging. Kaylee and Stephanie are basically like Sherlock and Watson on that TV show."

"Yeah, wasn't hard to find your social media profiles," Kaylee said with a shrug. "We read the comments your friends left, put two and two together. Shoplifting is like a *real* crime, you know."

The three girls stared at Dawn. Suddenly, despite their prim dresses and fancy shoes, they didn't look so nice anymore. The *nice* girls here were actually the *mean* girls, Dawn realized.

Not only that, but based on the other kids' reactions, they'd clearly spread the gossip around the whole school. Everyone seemed to be in on the joke. They all pointed and laughed at Dawn. It was worse than her terrible nightmare, because this was real life.

"Look at the new kid!" Dawn heard a girl whisper. "She's a criminal!"

A boy's voice rang out next. "She actually thought she was getting an invitation!"

The jeering voices and snickers cut through the hall.

Dawn spun around, feeling dizzy. The chant—"criminal"—reverberated down the hall, spreading like wildfire. Only one person wasn't laughing and whispering about her.

Phillipa watched her with a concerned expression. She was clutching one of her thick books. She shook her head sadly.

I'm so sorry, Phillipa mouthed.

So that was what Phillipa had meant the day before about not trusting Leah and her friends.

Dawn's stomach dropped at that realization. But she still felt like she could turn this whole situation around. She shot Leah a pleading look.

"Please, let me come to your birthday party," Dawn whispered in desperation. Her cheeks flamed and felt hot. "Listen, I'm new here. I don't know anyone. Please, I just . . . want a friend."

Dawn took a step toward Leah, but Leah looked appalled and cringed back in horror.

"No way!" Leah said, acting all innocent. "I'm not inviting a *common criminal* to my birthday party. What would everyone think?"

"But I'm not a common criminal," Dawn said, keeping her voice low. "It was all a big misunderstanding. I didn't steal anything."

"Oh yeah?" Leah said, folding her arms. "Then why did your parents send you away?"

That hit Dawn hard.

Why doesn't anyone ever believe me?

"Please, you can trust me," Dawn begged, feeling tears drip down her face. "I'm not a criminal. I'll prove it! Just let me come to your party."

"Not a chance," Leah said, flipping her hair back and pursing her lips in disdain. "You might steal something from my house. You're a bad influence."

"Her father is the mayor," Kaylee added. "Don't you get it?"

"Yeah, they have to be careful who they associate

with," Stephanie chimed in. "What would everyone think? We all know what you did."

With that, the girls spun around in a pack and floated together into the classroom, leaving Dawn alone in the hall. She felt more mortified than she ever had before in her entire life. This was even worse than when that security guard had caught her friends shoplifting.

She could hear everyone whispering and gossiping about her.

Did you hear what Leah said . . . she's a criminal . . . she stole from a store . . . arrested with her friends . . . her parents sent her away . . . they don't want her anymore . . .

Each whisper hit Dawn like a dagger to the heart. Words had power, like magic spells. They could wound you, maybe even kill you. *Can you die of embarrassment?* she wondered.

Ring!

Suddenly, the bell signaled that Dawn had to go to class, though she wanted to run as far away as possible and *never* speak to Leah or anyone in Castletown ever again.

This felt like déjà vu. No matter how hard she tried

to do the right thing, bad things always happened to her. They followed her like a curse.

But Dawn didn't have a choice.

Feeling hopeless, Dawn took her seat in the back next to Phillipa and hunched over, while Mr. Blankenship called the class to order. But every time his back was turned or he wasn't paying attention, she could hear her classmates whisper at her.

"*Shoplifted . . . stole from a store . . . bad influence . . . criminal.*"

Dawn shrank down further in her desk. Worse yet, she saw all the other kids in class clutching their invitations to Leah's party: pink envelopes sealed with a rose sticker with actual birthday invites inside them.

Leah's 13ᵗʰ Princess Birthday!

Every kid in the class except for Dawn had an invite. She clutched the nasty trick invitation in her hand, crumpling it up in her fist. It wasn't fair.

Even Phillipa clutched a party invite, though she shot Dawn a feeling-guilty look.

Then something worse happened.

Leah shot Dawn a smug look and mouthed, *You should be locked up in jail.*

That was it—Dawn couldn't take it anymore. Her mortification morphed into raging hot anger. Her blood started to simmer, then boil. Yeah, she had done some bad stuff, but jail? That was a whole other level and a complete exaggeration. The shoplifting incident, her parents blaming her when it wasn't her fault and sending her away, now this prank . . . it all erupted at once.

I'm being falsely accused, Dawn thought furiously.

Before she knew what she was doing, Dawn stood up from her seat and marched to the front of the room. It felt like someone else was controlling her. The anger just took over her body.

A hush fell over the class.

The kids stared at her in surprise.

Even Mr. Blankenship looked taken aback, but Dawn didn't give him a chance to speak.

She pointed her finger at Leah.

"You're a bully!" Dawn yelled. "How could you do this? You're a terrible person."

Shocked gasps shot through the class. Even Mr. Blankenship looked horrified.

"Oh my gosh, get her away from me!" Leah cried, leaping back and acting innocent. "Mr. Blankenship, help! She's trying to attack me!"

"You did this!" Dawn said, holding up the crumpled card with *CRIMINAL* written on it.

"What on earth?" Leah said innocently. "I've never seen that before in my life."

Dawn stared at her in disgust. She couldn't believe Leah could lie that easily.

Meanwhile, Kaylee and Stephanie came to Leah's defense. "Yeah, we heard the new girl got sent away from home because she was trouble," Kaylee said, taking up the innocent act.

"Mr. Blankenship," Stephanie interjected with a faux horrified expression, "the new girl probably wrote that herself to make Leah look bad."

The whole class gasped at the accusations.

"Okay, everyone, enough!" Mr. Blankenship said. He leaned over and studied the card. "Dawn, please return to your seat at once."

"But she did this!" Dawn started. "They're lying and spreading rumors about me—"

"Enough!" Mr. Blankenship cut her off. "Leah has had perfect attendance and grades all year. You expect me to believe that she would lie?"

Leah put on her most innocent face, but her eyes remained cold. Nobody believed Dawn because of her past. They all took Leah's side.

"But it's not fair—" Dawn started.

"That's it, you're going to the principal's office," Mr. Blankenship said. "I can't have you disturbing my class."

He pointed to the door. The whole class fell silent, while Leah just shot her a smug look.

Criminal, she mouthed one last time. *You deserve to get punished.*

* * *

"Young lady, have a seat," the secretary chirped from reception, pointing into the dark office beyond. It looked foreboding, giving Dawn a bad feeling. "Principal Hubert will be in shortly."

Through the windows in the reception office's door,

Dawn could see into the hall on the other side. The principal was having a heated conversation with Mr. Blankenship. Her teacher was gesturing around. His cheeks were aflame. He looked angry. That was another bad sign.

Dawn pulled her eyes away and sulked as she headed into the office. She plopped onto the sofa, feeling completely alone and misunderstood. Soon that dissolved into anger, which quickly melted into regret. She was supposed to be on her best behavior. That was the only way she was getting back home. Why did this always happen to her?

Dawn stared at the framed picture on the wall. It was a sad, drooping map of Castletown. It showed the tiny town center, with even Spindles 'N' Things marked on it. The antique shop had been there for . . . well . . . longer than Dawn had been alive. The map also depicted the sprawling forest and the mountains. Dawn stared at the sharp peaks painted onto the parchment.

Forbidden Mountains, the map read. That made Dawn shudder.

Principal Hubert entered the office and closed the door behind her. She wore a navy pantsuit that was baggy and ill-fitting, yet still gave her an authoritative air. Her face was round and soft, but her eyes were dark and sharp. They fixed on Dawn and narrowed.

Dawn shrank down again—though now in a different place—awaiting her punishment. Despite the *incident* back home, this was the first time she'd actually been sent to the principal's office. It was just as horrible as she'd imagined.

But it was Principal Hubert's expression—*frowning, accusing*—and the way she sat behind her desk—*staring her down like she was guilty*—that made it horrible.

Dawn felt her stomach curl and clench. She swallowed against it, but her mouth tasted like sandpaper.

A long moment passed. It felt like an eternity.

"Young lady, I spoke to Mr. Blankenship," Principal Hubert said. "I don't know what your old school up north was like, but this behavior is unacceptable in Castletown. Is that understood?"

"Yes, ma'am," Dawn whispered. Her voice seemed to have deserted her. She didn't bother defending herself. Nobody here believed her. Leah was too good of a liar.

Principal Hubert picked up the phone and dialed it.

Tap. Tap. Tap. Tap-tap-tap-tap.

Dawn heard her aunt's tinny voice echo out of the

receiver. "Spindles 'N' Things!" she chirped cheerfully. "How can I help you today?"

"This is Principal Hubert."

Dawn sank lower in her chair.

"I regret to inform you," started Principal Hubert, speaking into the receiver, "there was an incident at school today involving your niece. You might want to sit down."

That was when Dawn's ears started to ring, and she didn't hear anything else after that. She just felt dread. Her aunts were certain to inform her parents that she had got in trouble . . . again. And they wouldn't believe that it wasn't her fault.

While a worried voice leaked out of the phone—from her aunt, of course—and the principal droned on about the incident that day, the desire for revenge ignited in Dawn's heart with black fire.

The flames grew stronger and darker. Because of Leah, Dawn was stuck here, and she might never get to go back home. One thought flashed through her head, feeding the flames. They burned hotter and blacker.

Leah deserved to get punished for what she had done.

5
MAJOR FOMO

ing!

The bell jingled over the door, as Dawn returned from sweeping the front stoop and cleaning the windows. Her arms ached and her feet were tired, but she didn't dare complain. Not after what had happened at school. Despite her efforts to erase the morning's events from her memory, they haunted her.

Principal Hubert's voice still rang in her ears. *This behavior is unacceptable at Castletown.*

Usually chatty and chipper, her aunts had barely spoken to her since they picked her up. Dawn wanted to tell them that it wasn't her fault.

But from experience, she knew that defending herself

would get her into more trouble. Nobody would believe her side of the story. She'd learned that the hard way when her parents sent her away. Anger stoked her heart like the wood-fired stove in her aunts' kitchen. It fueled her desire for revenge. Each flicker said . . .

This is so unfair. . . . Leah is a liar. . . .

Her aunts still hadn't called her parents . . . yet. But she knew it was coming. She could feel it inching closer with each passing minute. The dread ate away at her, making her feel sick to her stomach.

Dawn picked her way through the store's cluttered aisles, carting her broom and cleaning supplies. Her eyes swept over the reclaimed fragments of other people's lives. Porcelain dolls and toys from another generation, fancy tea sets, souvenir silver spoons, and all manner of worn furniture. There was even a rack of old sunglasses by the register.

Dawn grabbed a pair and tried them on for fun, frowning through the scratched lenses. She set them back, turned around, and accidentally thrust her face into the bouquets of roses on the checkout counter. She caught a big whiff—

"Achoo!"

"Dearie, is that you?'

It was Aunt Fleur. "Oh, dang it, I thought perhaps it might be a customer," Fleur said, letting out a deep sigh. "I heard the bell and got my hopes up."

"Sorry, just me," Dawn said. She scratched her nose. It itched terribly now that she was in proximity to the roses again.

"Well, if you're all finished with the front . . ." Aunt Fleur went on, her voice sounding deflated. She was disappointed in her niece, Dawn could tell. But more than that, she seemed worried about the shop. "We'd like you to clean the shed out back."

"The shed?" Dawn said.

That sounded *extra* dusty.

"Yes," Fleur said. "It could use a proper cleaning."

"Oh, dearie, do be careful out there," Aunt Merry added, popping out of the back office. She clutched an overflowing ledger of receipts and expenses. Her face was pinched with worry.

"Uh, what do you mean?" Dawn asked.

"Well, most of that inventory hasn't been touched

in eons," Fleur chimed in. "It's stuff we picked up in bulk at estate auctions."

"But you never know," Merry said, raising her eyebrows hopefully. "Something valuable might be stashed back there."

"Yes, ma'am," Dawn said.

She wasn't sure what *eons* meant, only that it sounded like an awful long time. That meant she'd be sneezing her way through another afternoon of chores.

* * *

Dawn stood in front of the door to the shed. It was a derelict aluminum-sided building shoved in the back of the parking lot. It looked dimly lit, ghostly, and rundown. She felt both grossed out and a little bit afraid of what lurked inside.

But she had to do her chores. Dawn reached for the door and yanked it open—

Caw! Caw! Caw!

Black shadows with wings swarmed out at her. Their razor-sharp claws swiped for her face.

"No, get away!" Dawn yelled, leaping back in fear as the cruel intentions of the ravens burst out.

The birds screamed and screeched, sounding like demons, upset that she'd disturbed their dwelling.

Caw! Caw! Caw!

One scratched her cheek, just missing her eye and drawing blood. It stung and made her cry a little bit in pain.

"Get away, you hideous creatures!" Dawn yelped, grabbing her broom for protection.

She waved it at the ravens, shooing them away from the shed. Black feathers swirled in the air around her like dark snowfall. Her adversaries screamed in outrage.

But then, fortunately, they dispersed and flew toward the forest on the other side of town.

Dawn reached up and touched her face. The cut was shallow and not serious. Her aunts had warned her about old junk being stored in the unit, but they hadn't said anything about evil birds.

I hate nature, Dawn thought in annoyance.

The door to the shed creaked, swaying in the wind

and banging into the surrounding aluminum siding. Dawn peered at the interior. Light slanted through the dingy crud-caked windows, making the dust swirl in an elaborate dance.

If the actual shop was cluttered, then the shed was overrun with junk. Nothing was organized. Things were just piled in heaps. Dawn studied the first items she came to: creepy dolls, frayed furniture, chipped teacups, and kitchen stuff. Most of the artifacts were broken or stained or useless. Or all three.

How long has it been here?

Dawn began sifting through the piles and attempting to sort them. The deeper she got into the shed, the stranger the items became. Some looked like they'd been stashed back there for . . . well . . . *eons*!

Medieval tapestries, dusty and obscured, hung on the walls. She also discovered a rusty sword with a bejeweled hilt, a tattered baby carrier, and stacks of old books with weathered spines and yellowing pages.

One tapestry depicted a black dragon breathing emerald fire—and roses snaking up a castle wall like weeds. A handsome brown-haired prince battled the dragon, clutching a sword. Dawn picked up the sword she found and studied the elaborate hilt.

Sword of Truth was emblazoned on it. She wondered if it was the same one in the tapestry, but quickly dismissed that thought. If anything, it was probably a fake. Everything back there was old junk that nobody wanted, right?

After wading through to the back of the shed dusty and exhausted, Dawn slumped down on the floor and fished out her phone. She miraculously got a signal out there, of all places.

Feeling her heart race, Dawn flipped to her social media profile, scanning the posts and pics. She navigated to the page for her new middle school and spotted Leah's name. She hesitated, then clicked on it, even though she knew it was a bad idea.

Pictures from Leah's birthday party flooded the screen. Dawn scrolled through them. The party was princess-themed, with fancy cakes and treats piled on a table, dancing and karaoke, and even a pool out back, where kids swam and partied.

The party looked like a total blast. Everyone from her class was having the best time—and here Dawn was . . .

alone, miserable, and sulking her way through a dusty shed, surrounded by creepy, vicious birds; worthless junk; and who knew what other horrors.

But she couldn't help it. She kept scrolling through vids and pics of Leah's party, feeling worse and worse with each refresh. Leah wore a bright pink party dress and clutched a bouquet of red roses. A golden crown sat atop her flowing blond hair.

All their classmates surrounded her and sang happy birthday, as a huge cake shaped like a castle with thirteen candles was brought out. Leah closed her eyes, made a wish, and blew them all out with one breath. Everyone cheered. The caption under the vid read *Hail to the Princess*, followed by crown emojis.

Tears pricked Dawn's eyes, making the vid go blurry.

How dare Leah do this to her? She had major FOMO. It just wasn't fair. That was what she got for trying to do the right thing and follow the rules for once. Clearly, that was a big mistake.

Dawn started sobbing angry tears. She kicked the heap of junk next to her—

Smash!

The pile almost collapsed on top of her. Dawn leapt back just in time to avoid being buried. "Oh, no," she thought, as it crashed to the ground and scattered around her.

If her aunts found out, she'd get in even more trouble.

Once the dust cleared, Dawn reached to pick up the stuff, shoving her hand into the nearest stack, when suddenly—

"Ouch!" she cried out.

Something sharp had stabbed her finger.

She sifted through the pile, unearthing . . . an antique spinning wheel. It had a bench seat, a wooden wheel, and a spindle. Despite its age, the spindle was still needle sharp.

Dawn looked at her fingertip. A drop of blood oozed out where she'd pricked it. The blood trickled down and hit the ground—

Caw! Caw!

Suddenly, ravens burst into the shed, swirling around her and diving at her head.

Dawn raised her arms and ducked down. Their feathers tickled her skin, making her squirm. But then, something far worse happened. . . .

Green flames exploded out of the spinning wheel, lighting up the shed with emerald fire. The heat hit Dawn's body, searing her skin. Everything was going to go up in flames.

Fear shot through Dawn. She grabbed her phone to call the fire department, but then lowered it slowly. . . .

Somehow, nothing else in the shed was catching on fire.

What kind of fire is this?

The unnatural flames licked at the spinning wheel, but it didn't burn. Even stranger, there was no smoke, either—just the sensation of heat wafting off it.

"Wh-what's happening?" Dawn stammered.

Suddenly, a terrible laugh reverberated out of the fire.

"Who . . . who's there?" Dawn gasped.

The flames exploded into the shape of a tall woman with a long black-and-purple robe that peaked into a sharp collar.

Dawn stared at her in shock. She had pale green skin, long spindly fingers tapering into spikey nails that could easily serve as weapons, and a pair of razor-sharp horns cresting her head, giving her a horrifying and supernatural appearance. Her face was elongated, almost unnatural, ending in a pointy chin.

Even more unnerving were her eyes. They glowed with pale yellow fire—and fixed on Dawn. The woman had an icy beauty to her, Dawn thought, a strange but alluring combination. She wielded a long staff crowned by a glowing crystal orb. Her deep voice echoed out:

"Who dares summon me?"

6

THE NOBILITY, THE
GENTRY, THE RABBLE

"Wh-who are you?" asked Dawn, backing away in fear.

Suddenly, one of the largest ravens swooped down and landed.

Caw! Caw!

The silhouette of the women stared back at Dawn. The raven cocked its head, regarding her, too. The spinning wheel continued to smolder with emerald flames. A drop of Dawn's blood still clung to the spindle.

Then, in a dramatic gesture, the woman lifted her arms. The robes made them look almost like wings. She cackled again. The raven joined in, cawing loudly.

The emerald flames licked higher. Dawn started to

sweat. The dark horned shadow loomed over her. She brought her staff down—*smack*—making the raven caw and flap its wings.

Her voice echoed out of the fire.

"My true name is Maleficent," she said in a commanding voice.

"What . . . what are you?" Dawn ventured.

"Ah, so many questions for such a little girl," Maleficent trilled, running her fingers over the raven's head. It leaned into her strokes. "But if you must know . . . I'm a fairy."

"How is that possible?" Dawn asked.

Maleficent bowed her head. "Many ages ago, I lost my spinning wheel. It was stolen and hidden from me. Now that I've been summoned, I want it back."

Dawn blinked at her in confusion. Everything felt so unreal—*so impossible*—and so terribly frightening. She kept expecting it to be another bad dream, like the nightmare she had about the roses. But every time her eyes popped open, the woman was still there.

She tried pinching herself—but still the dark fairy remained. The emerald flames and the raven also stayed put. Dawn didn't know what else to do, so she spoke . . . carefully.

"But how . . . did you find me?" Dawn asked, still trying to process what she was seeing and hearing.

"Your *blood*," Maleficent said, gesturing to the spindle. "When you pricked your finger, the dark magic summoned me here. It wasn't on purpose, then?"

Dawn peered down at her finger. A pinprick of blood still graced the tip. Understanding washed over her. So, that was what had summoned Maleficent!

"You want the spinning wheel?" she asked.

"Yes, it's infused with a great deal of my power," Maleficent said in a slightly bored voice, as if she were speaking to someone beneath her.

"Then why don't you just take it?" Dawn asked with a frown.

Maleficent just shook her head. "Even my powers have limits. Those simple fools cursed the wheel with powerful protection spells. If I try that, the curse will kill me."

Curse? Protection spells? That all sounded . . . ominous. Dawn's heart thumped faster, and she felt herself wanting to run away out of the shed.

But something else kept her frozen there. It was curiosity, she realized. The powerful contrasting emotions battled in her heart.

Dawn needed to know more. Plus, she wasn't totally sure that what she was seeing was actually real.

Finally, she found her voice. It trembled, but it was clear enough.

"Well, then how do you get the wheel back?" Dawn asked the fairy.

"It must be willingly given to me by the *owner* of the spinning wheel," Maleficent responded, tapping her fingers on her staff impatiently.

"The owner?" Dawn said, feeling unsure.

"Yes, and that appears to be . . . *you*."

"Me?" Dawn said, backing away.

Sure, she'd discovered the spinning wheel. But did that mean it belonged to her? Technically, didn't it belong to her aunts? If she gave it away, wasn't that stealing?

The *incident* flashed through her head. She couldn't afford to get in trouble again.

The fairy's voice snapped her back to attention.

"You discovered it, did you not?" Maleficent said

peevishly. "You summoned me here? So clearly that means the wheel belongs to you."

"I guess so," Dawn said, biting her lip.

"Then hand it over and let's get done with this," Maleficent said. Her patience was clearly wearing thin. And so was the raven's; it flapped its wings in anger.

Dawn glanced at the wheel again. Green flames still smoldered, making it look dangerous to touch. Like a warning. Her whole body shivered with fear, despite the searing heat coming from the flames.

This is blood magic, she realized.

That couldn't be a good thing. She started to back away slowly toward the door. Maleficent's eyes flashed with anger, but then the fairy got ahold of herself.

Her whole demeanor changed, as if she wished to lure Dawn back toward her. She spoke in a measured voice, devoid of the irritation it had possessed only a moment before.

"Oh, come now, why so melancholy?" Maleficent asked.

The voice drew Dawn's attention, and she found herself wanting to stay longer. Was this a spell? Or simply a manipulation? Regardless, Maleficent sounded soothing and hypnotic. Suddenly, Dawn felt her fears melting away. All thoughts of retreating vanished from her mind.

"What happened to you?" Maleficent went on in the same calm voice, her expression kind and understanding. "My child, I can sense your sadness."

Could the fairy read her mind?

Dawn knew that she shouldn't say anything. She should get her aunts and tell them about the wheel and the flames and how she had pricked her finger—

But something stopped her.

Revenge simmered in her heart. Nobody in Castletown believed her about Leah, but something told her that this fairy just might.

"It's this girl . . . at my new school," Dawn heard herself confessing, despite her earlier trepidation. "She played a cruel trick on me and didn't invite me to her birthday party today."

The fairy gasped in sympathy.

"My dear precious girl, you must feel quite distressed not receiving an invitation," Maleficent hissed, bringing her staff down.

Dawn was surprised. That was exactly how she felt! How did this fairy understand all that?

"Yeah, she invited everybody in my class and told people I was a criminal," Dawn went on, feeling the words tumbling from her lips.

Maleficent brought her hand to her chest in horror. "She invited everyone? The nobility, the gentry . . . even the rabble? And then she called you names?"

Dawn sniffled and nodded, finally feeling like somebody in this awful place understood her.

"Not getting invited to a party is something I know a little bit about," Maleficent said. "If you return my spinning wheel, I'll help you teach that poor simple fool a lesson."

Dawn was excited, but then she hesitated. "I don't know if that's such a good idea. Her father is the mayor . . . and she's like a princess here."

Maleficent cackled, raising her arms so her robe resembled wings.

"Even princesses need to be taught lessons," the fairy explained. "And the rest of the party rabble, too. I can make sure they pay for what they did to you."

Dawn still felt unsure. Wasn't revenge a bad thing? But then she remembered the social media posts and how Leah treated her. She could still hear her classmates' jeering laughter—*Criminal!*—and Leah's lies. Before Dawn knew what she was doing, her lips started moving. The words spilled out, fueled by the fire simmering darkly in her heart.

"Help me teach Leah and her friends a lesson," Dawn said in a loud, clear voice. She met the fairy's eyes. "And I'll give you the spinning wheel back. But not yet . . ."

Maleficent's eyebrow arched in surprise. "What do you mean, child?"

That was when Dawn's street smarts kicked in. She'd learned a lot of lessons growing up in the city. She had to be sure that the fairy could actually do what she promised and, most importantly, that she would keep her end of the bargain.

Dawn held the fairy's gaze. She didn't back down or show any weakness. For the first time since she'd arrived, she started to feel like her old self.

"First, you have to prove to me that you can punish Leah and those kids for what they did," Dawn said.

Standing up to the fairy was terrifying, but she forced herself to continue. "Then, I'll give you the spinning wheel back. Do we have a deal?"

Caw! Caw!

Maleficent's trusted raven screeched as it flapped its wings.

Then, the cackle echoed out again. Dawn shuddered at the sound.

"After the sun sets on her thirteenth birthday tonight," Maleficent proclaimed, "so it shall be granted. You'll see the proof, I promise. Then, you must bring me the spinning wheel before the sun sets again tomorrow night. Do you understand?"

Dawn couldn't back out, not now.

"Yes, I agree," she said. And then—

The dark fairy raised her staff and brought it down. *Crack!* The noise echoed through the shed. The raven took off. The flames erupted higher; then, in a puff of smoke, the fairy vanished, sucked back into the spinning wheel.

Emerald flames shot out and engulfed Dawn's body.

She collapsed to the ground and writhed around, trying to put them out. The raven kept cawing and circling her.

She couldn't breathe suddenly . . . it was just like she was suffocating.

What did I just do? Dawn thought dimly through the searing pain enveloping her whole body. When the fairy vanished, it was like whatever magic spell had made Dawn trust her evaporated, too. Fear rushed back in its place, coupled with something worse . . . regret.

Her vision dimmed and then—

Everything went black.

7

SPINDLE YOUR WHEELS

As the fire receded, Dawn came out of her trance. She blinked in shock, trying to remember what had happened.

The dark fairy's cackling voice still echoed in her ears. *After the sun sets on her thirteenth birthday tonight . . . so it shall be granted.*

She felt a shiver creep down her spine. But now, as the fading afternoon light slanted through the dingy windows, it just looked like a harmless old spinning wheel. Nothing was out of place.

No fairy, no flames, and no—

Caw! Caw!

Dawn jumped.

Okay, the raven was still there. That was real. The bird took off from the rafters, madly flapping its wings.

Dawn thrust open the doors, and the raven flew out. It vanished into the dark forest, swallowed up by the thick trees.

Suddenly, the wind kicked up, whistling into the shed and rocking the doors.

Smack!

They slammed back toward Dawn. She leapt to the side to avoid getting hit. *Okay, that was kind of freaky.*

Slowly, she retreated, still feeling startled, and thought about everything that had just happened. Dark fairies? Blood magic? Emerald flames? Magical spinning wheels and curses? It had to be her overactive imagination, right? Too much time spent isolated, out in the middle of nowhere, with zero social life and limited Internet connectivity would make any teen go nuts.

This was the stuff of fairy tales and legends, or books like the ones Phillipa read. It wasn't real life.

Still feeling uncertain, Dawn swept her gaze over the shed. A lone shaft of light shone down on the spinning wheel through the slits in the wooden shutters.

"You're not magical," Dawn whispered to it. "You're just a piece of old junk."

She ran her hand over the antique to reassure herself, feeling the splinters poking out of the weathered old wood. She turned the wheel, which gave way stubbornly, however slowly. But the spindle remained almost as if new, with a dot of her blood still gracing its tip.

She glanced down at her hurt finger. Her eyes widened: it was healed and the skin was unbroken. There was no sign that she'd injured it.

Dawn felt a shudder echo through her body. Goose bumps pricked her skin.

How had that happened? How was it already healed?

But there was nothing supernatural about the spinning wheel. It looked like the rest of the stuff crammed in the shed—old rubbish that nobody in their right mind would ever want.

Especially a dark fairy, right?

Dawn shook her head at how ridiculous that idea

sounded. She couldn't tell anyone about what she'd imagined.

Suddenly, another voice hit her ears. This one was friendlier.

"Dearie, are you finished in there?"

It was Aunt Merry.

"Sun's setting," Aunt Fleur added in a singsong voice. "We should close up the shop, get home and fix up some supper."

Dawn relaxed slightly. "Almost finished!" she called back, grabbing for supplies.

She set back to work, sifting through the junk. To her delight, she found an ancient bicycle and dusted it off. It was old-fashioned and cherry red. It even had a basket strapped to the back and a silver bell that chimed when she flicked it. She reattached the chain, then tried the pedals. She wheeled the bike outside and gave it a test run. Amazingly, the bike worked perfectly. She did a few laps in the parking lot. Maybe she could convince her aunts to let her keep it. She might not have the subway here, but a bicycle meant one thing: *freedom*.

She wouldn't be stuck at home or dependent on her

aunts to give her rides. Plus, she had been dreading riding the bus to school the next morning with the other kids because of the rumors and gossip. This way, she could bike to school instead. Then after school, she could ride to the antique shop to help her aunts out. It would save them the trip.

Cheered up, Dawn propped the bike by the front door. Then she decided to take advantage of her phone signal and shoot a quick text to her old friends, telling them about her disaster of a day. They'd never play a cruel trick on her like Leah had.

But when she opened her phone, it still showed the pictures of the party. New images had been uploaded since she last checked, bringing a fresh swell of rage to Dawn's heart. She felt attacked by the posts. The problems didn't stop at the end of the school day, thanks to her phone and social media. Now they could haunt her all through the night.

Forlorn, she put down her phone, not even bothering to text Ronnie and Daniella. She didn't have the heart to rehash it all. She just wanted to forget everything that had happened—including the weird waking nightmare about the fairy in the shed. She wished it was as easy to turn off her brain as it was to put away her phone.

* * *

That night after work, Dawn shoveled some dinner—a strange sort of thick stew with chicken and dumplings that made her miss pizza—into her mouth and choked out a question.

"So, uh, did you talk to my parents yet?" Dawn mumbled.

Her aunts exchanged worried looks. Their arms fluttered slightly. "Not yet, dearie," Fleur said finally. Her voice sounded heavy.

"Tomorrow," Merry added with a sigh. "No use putting it off anymore."

That meant Dawn had one last night before her parents found out.

Her appetite evaporated instantly, as her stomach churned and sloshed. She set her spoon down and announced that she was tired.

"Best get your beauty rest," Merry said, clearing her bowl and taking it to the sink.

"Rest up. Tomorrow is a new day," Fleur added, trying to sound hopeful.

But Dawn could tell that they weren't relishing delivering this news to her parents. It weighed on them, too. But it was inevitable, just like her having to face her classmates at school the next day.

Dawn wished her aunts good night, then trudged up the creaky stairs and headed off to bed.

She quickly fell into a restless sleep. She tossed and turned, tussling with the quilt. "Common criminal!" Leah's cruel taunt echoed in her head. Shadows chased her through the school halls, yelling that at her and snickering at her.

"No, please . . . it's all a big mistake!" Dawn whimpered, cowering down and trying to hide. "I didn't steal anything! I swear . . . I'm not a criminal!"

But the shadows chased her anyway. She ran down the hall into a room where she slammed the door—and suddenly, she was somewhere else altogether.

She was back in the shed. She blinked in confusion. Ravens swarmed all around, cawing and dive-bombing her. One pricked her shoulder, while another scratched her cheeks.

"No, get away!"

The spinning wheel sat in the back. A shaft of light shone down on it. But then . . . *creak . . . creak . . . creak . . .* the wheel started to spin on its own accord.

How was that possible?

Dawn backed away. Her heart was threatening to beat out of her chest

Out of the wheel poured golden yarn, woven seemingly from thin air and spun into thread. The thread piled up on the floor, as it spun faster and faster.

Clank, clank.

And then—

The thread shot out at Dawn!

She tried to run away, but the thread wrapped around her ankles and tripped her. She fell hard onto the dusty floor. Her eyes watered from the pain. She struggled to get free. . . .

"No, let me go . . . please!" she gasped.

But it was futile.

The thread came alive like a snake and climbed up her legs, wrapped around her torso, her arms, and finally reached her neck. It encircled it, and then the end of the thread rose as if it was looking at her. It swayed back and forth in front of her eyes.

"No, let me go!" Dawn cried, but her voice was cut off as the thread twisted tighter around her.

Suddenly, the thread slithered into her mouth and down her throat.

Dawn tried to breathe but gagged and gasped for air. She felt the thread relentlessly sliding down her throat, wriggling *inside* her.

A dark shadow rose over her, as she writhed around on the floor. The eyes glowed with yellow light, boring into her.

Then, a hideous cackle echoed out.

"After sunset tomorrow!" the voice boomed. "That wheel belongs to me!"

8
SLEEPING BEAUTY

"No, let me go!"

Dawn woke with a start, gasping for air. She clawed at her throat . . . but then lowered her hands. Nothing was wrapped around her except the quilt. Early-morning light leaked into her room. She was safe in her bed.

It was just another terrible nightmare.

If only yesterday could be a terrible nightmare, she thought, *one that you woke up from like it had never happened at all.*

But it wasn't. And that day, her parents were going to find out about it.

Groggy, Dawn got ready for school and trudged down the stairs. The steps groaned with each footfall, like her sore muscles. A night of tossing and turning, on top of cleaning the shed, had left her whole body aching.

Dawn took a breath and headed into the kitchen, waiting for the bad news that her aunts had already spoken to her parents.

"There's our sleeping beauty!"

Dawn shot them a weird look, taken aback by their extra-cheerful tone. She still expected to be in trouble.

But they seemed . . . happy. How was that possible?

"Uh, yes," Dawn said. "I'm awake, or at least I think I am."

Aunt Merry tittered and then exchanged looks with her wife. "Well, we woke up extra early and decided to swing by the shop."

"Uh, you did?" Dawn asked, still unsure how this changed their attitude toward her.

"We took a lil' gander at the shed," Fleur said. "It looks the best it has in . . . well . . . eons!"

They both chuckled.

"Well, it took a lot of work," Dawn said. "It was pretty filthy back there. Not to mention all the ravens."

"But there's more, dearie," Fleur chirped, shooting her wife a conspiratorial look.

Dawn frowned. "What's that?"

"The spinning wheel!" they exclaimed at once.

"What about it?" Dawn asked in confusion. She had a vague memory of finding a spinning wheel, but like her creepy nightmare the night before, it was already fading fast.

Still, a bad feeling lingered in the pit of her stomach, making it churn.

"My dear, it's a valuable antique," Aunt Merry explained. "Folks love collecting medieval relics like that."

"That's right," Fleur said. "We're going to make a load of money selling it. We already called the auction house, and they verified it."

"It's been a real struggle for us lately," Merry said, putting her arm around her wife's shoulders. "But with this rare find, we should be able to keep it running."

"That's right! You've saved our shop," Fleur said. Then both aunts swept her into a hug.

Dawn hesitated. Through her fuzzy memories, she could recall promising to give the spinning wheel back to a dark fairy, but she shook that off. This was the first truly good thing that had happened to her since she got to Castletown. She basked in the praise of her aunts.

Fleur and Merry hugged her tighter.

"We knew letting you come live with us was a great idea," Merry said.

"We're so happy to have you here," Fleur added. "And we can't wait to tell your parents."

Dawn pulled back slightly and looked down at her shoes, feeling terrible. "What about. . . what happened at school yesterday?"

"Oh, silly, fiddle-faddle," Fleur said. "That can be our lil' secret."

"Water under the bridge," Merry said with a dismissive wave of her hand.

"What . . . do you mean?" Dawn asked in surprise. "You're not going to tell them?"

"You've saved our shop," Merry said. "We can do something to save you, too."

"Wait, you mean it?" Dawn said, feeling like an enormous weight had been lifted off her shoulders.

"Of course, dearie," Merry said.

Her aunts tittered, and for the first time in a long while, Dawn felt herself smiling, too. A real smile, not a fake one.

Dawn forced away all thoughts of returning the spinning wheel to the fairy. Fairies weren't real. Neither were bewitched spinning wheels.

But saving her aunts' shop—that was something real. The spinning wheel was her "get out of parental jail free" card, and she was going to play it.

9
AFTER THE SUN SETS

As a reward for Dawn's hard work and finding the spinning wheel, her aunts let her keep the old bike she had found in the shed and ride it to school instead of making her take the bus. But as soon as she got off her bike, her good mood vanished. Leah was right ahead of her with Kaylee and Stephanie. They were holding up their phones, showing each other pictures and social media posts from the party.

Dawn shrank back. And it didn't get any better when she got to class. All the kids were standing around, waiting for the bell to ring and sharing stories about the party.

"Last night was rad," Kaylee said, thrusting her phone

at Leah. "Oh my gosh, it was the single greatest party of all time! Look at all the *likes* you're getting."

"Yeah, it was epic," Leah said with a smug smile.

Then, her eyes landed on Dawn.

"Too bad the *criminal* couldn't come," she said in a low voice so the teacher couldn't hear.

Dawn locked eyes with Leah. She felt that fire burn in her heart for revenge. It grew hotter . . . and hotter . . . and then the strangest thing happened.

Leah stumbled, almost falling over into her desk. She barely caught herself.

Her friends jumped to her aid.

"Oh, no, are you okay?" Kaylee asked in alarm.

"Leah, what's wrong?" Stephanie said.

"Oh my, I'm so dizzy," Leah slurred, leaning into her desk. "And so . . . sleepy."

Dawn watched them in shock. Had she caused that to happen?

No way, she decided. Her thoughts didn't have power.

"Do you need to go to the school nurse?" Kaylee asked.

Leah waved her off. "No, I'll be fine. It's just a fainting spell or something. Just let me sit down and rest up."

"Probably sugar-crashing from all that cake," Kaylee said. "I know the feeling. I've been tired all morning. I didn't even want to get up."

"Yeah," Stephanie added. "Come to think of it, I'm pretty sleepy, too." She stifled a yawn, then sat down.

Kaylee also sat down with a yawn. "Yeah, I need a nap ASAP."

It was as if the yawns were contagious. Soon, all the kids in class were yawning and rubbing their eyes. That was strange, Dawn thought.

"Hey, new kid," Phillipa said, sliding into the desk next to Dawn's. "How ya doing?"

"Okay, I guess," Dawn said. "Do you notice how tired everyone is today?"

Phillipa shrugged. "Probably cuz the party went super late or something. I wouldn't know."

"Wait, what do you mean?" Dawn asked. "Weren't you there, too?"

"I didn't feel like going," Phillipa said. She caught Dawn's eye. "Not after what Leah did to you yesterday."

"Wow, I don't know what to say," Dawn said, feeling more cheerful. "I thought the whole class went to the party except for me."

"Well, not everyone here is like that, you know," Phillipa said, wiping her hands on her dusty coveralls. "You've got a friend . . . if you want one."

"Of course I do!" Dawn said right away, not even bothering to try to play it cool.

Before they could talk further, Mr. Blankenship called the class to order. As he began their first lesson, Dawn heard . . . *snoring*.

It was loud and growing louder.

Her eyes shot toward where it was coming from. It was Leah.

She was slumped forward with her head down on her desk, snoring away through class. Then Dawn heard giggling rippling through the class. Mr. Blankenship wheeled around.

"Leah, what on earth?" he said in surprise.

"Uh, where am I?" Leah gasped, sitting up with a start.

The class exploded in laughter. They were all

laughing . . . at Leah. Dawn couldn't help it: she felt satisfaction. This was what Leah deserved.

"You're in my class," Mr. Blankenship said in a stern voice. "And you fell asleep."

"Oh, I did?" Leah said, slipping into her innocent voice.

"Stay awake—or I'll have to send you home," Mr. Blankenship said. It seemed like Leah's star-student act wasn't working so well that day. "Now back to the fall of Rome . . ."

He continued teaching their history lesson on the Middle Ages. But soon . . . the snoring started again. And this time it was even louder.

Leah couldn't stay awake.

But it wasn't just Leah. Soon, all who had attended the party—practically the entire class—had their heads down on their desks. Many of them had fallen asleep and were snoring, too. It created a cacophony of noise.

Dawn couldn't believe her luck. She and Phillipa were the only two not falling asleep.

"What's gotten into y'all today?" Mr. Blankenship said in an irate voice.

But even that chastising missive didn't wake them up. They were all in a deep sleep. The snoring continued unabated.

"Leah, wake up!" Mr. Blankenship said, going over to prod her arm.

She bolted upright. "I'm awake . . . I'm awake!" But then she put her head back down and immediately fell asleep again.

"That's it, I'm fetching the nurse," Mr. Blankenship said. He scanned the class, his eyes landing on Dawn and Phillipa.

"You two are in charge until I'm back," Mr. Blankenship said, "seeing as you're the only students *awake* today. I know school isn't as exciting as YouTube, but this is ridiculous."

"Mr. Blankenship, they're probably tired from the party," Phillipa said.

"What do you mean?" Mr. Blankenship said, narrowing his eyes.

"Me and Dawn are the only two kids who didn't go to Leah's birthday party last night," Phillipa went on. "I bet they stayed up too late."

"That figures," Mr. Blankenship said. "Guess I'll be fetching Principal Hubert, too."

With that, he hurried from the class. Dawn was elated. Could this day go any better?

"Serves her right," Dawn said to Phillipa. "Now I'm glad I didn't get invited."

"You can say that again," Phillipa said.

Soon, Mr. Blankenship returned with the nurse and Principal Hubert in tow. The principal took one look at the class; then her face turned red.

"Well, in all my years," she said, shaking her head, "I've never seen such a sorry sight."

"Let's phone their parents and get them straight home," the nurse said, "so they can sleep it off."

"You're right," Principal Hubert agreed. "No use keeping them here. A party, huh?"

"That's apparently what happened," Mr. Blankenship agreed, pursing his lips in disapproval. "Leah's birthday. And on a school night. Looks like it went extra late."

The principal turned to Dawn and Phillipa. "Well, at least you've got two good students."

Dawn beamed at the principal's praise.

AFTER THE SUN SETS

The rest of class was amazing. Mr. Blankenship sat with Dawn and Phillipa instead of lecturing from the front of the room. He told them all kinds of fantastical stories about various medieval kings and queens who ruled over Europe during the Dark Ages.

"You're both getting an extra-credit A for today," Mr. Blankenship said right before the bell rang to release them from school.

As Dawn hurried toward the door, Mr. Blankenship stopped her.

"Listen, I'm sorry about yesterday," he said. "I know coming to a new school can be tough. I should've listened to your side of the story and not jumped to conclusions. Even teachers make mistakes."

"Uh, thanks," Dawn said, unable to believe her luck. "Really, it means a lot."

"You're welcome!" Mr. Blankenship said. "See you tomorrow, Dawn."

* * *

Dawn skipped down the hall, catching up to Phillipa by the doors. Her friend—*wow, she had a friend here* —waved. Outside, the school buses idled in the parking lot.

"Hey, wanna come over today?" Phillipa said, mounting her bicycle to begin her ride home. "And play with Samson? He's my dog. He's super big and fluffy, but also super friendly."

"Oh, I'd love to," Dawn said. "But I've gotta work at the shop."

"Spindles 'N' Things?" Phillipa said.

"Yup, that's the place," Dawn said. "You been in there?"

"Who hasn't?" Phillipa said. "My mom loves antiques. You should see our house. It kind of looks like a castle, actually."

"Maybe tomorrow," Dawn said. "I'll ask if I can have the afternoon off."

"So weird what happened today, right?" Phillipa said, turning back on her bike. "How they all fell asleep like that?" She let out a low whistle. "Must've been some party."

Dawn gave her a heartfelt look. "That's cosmic revenge," she said, and Phillipa agreed but then seemed hesitant.

"Even so," Phillipa said, biting her lip, "hopefully they get better soon."

"Yes, of course," Dawn said quickly. "I'm sure they'll be fine after a full night of sleep," she added for good measure.

She waved while Phillipa biked off. This had already been the best day that she'd had in . . . well . . . eons.

Despite what she'd said to Phillipa, Dawn was secretly thrilled that Leah and her friends had suffered major consequences for their actions. Now Leah would learn her lesson and think twice about excluding Dawn or making fun of her.

Everything was going great for her finally. Her teacher believed her about what had happened the day before. Meantime, her aunts were thrilled with her for discovering the valuable antique spinning wheel. Feeling hopeful, she hopped on her bike and rode to work.

At the shop, her aunts even called her parents and raved about what a good job she was doing and what a hard worker she was.

"This spinning wheel could save our shop, and it's all thanks to Dawn!" they exclaimed into the phone.

They continued to pour out praise about her work ethic. She could hear her parents' proud voices echoing from the receiver, before they handed the phone over.

Dawn talked to them, while she watched her aunts carry the spinning wheel into the back office. Despite her parents' obvious joy at her progress in Castletown, something nagged at Dawn. Out of nowhere, a memory resurfaced from the day before.

The dark fairy's voice echoed in her head:

After the sun sets on her thirteenth birthday . . .

Could that be why Leah hadn't been able to stay awake that day? But Dawn quickly dismissed it.

Her aunts opened a large safe and placed the spinning wheel inside it. They carefully set it down. Suddenly—

The wheel flashed with emerald light.

Fear shot through Dawn. She blinked, trying to clear her vision. *Probably just a trick of the light reflecting off the spindle, right?* she thought, trying to reassure herself.

Before Dawn could worry further, her aunts shut the door to the safe and spun the lock, securing the wheel inside.

"Dawn, you there?" Mom asked, snapping Dawn out of her thoughts.

"Uh, yes . . . what were you saying?" Dawn asked, still feeling unsettled.

"We're so proud of you," her mother said. "We knew this was the best decision."

"Just keep it up," Dad added, "and you'll be back home before you know it. We miss you!"

"And we love you!" Mom said.

Before Dawn fell asleep that night, snuggled into her bed under the quilt, she texted Ronnie and Daniella all the good news. They texted back right away.

DAWN: *At this rate, I'll be home before you know it! And we can have that party.* 🎈🎈🎈

DANIELLA: *Oh, can't wait. It'll be the best party ever. We miss you!*

RONNIE: *Hurry back! It's seriously not the same without you.*

10
THE FORBIDDEN MOUNTAINS

But the next day at school, Dawn's eyes fell on a mostly empty classroom. She gasped.

Mr. Blankenship sat at his desk, but there was no sign of Leah or any of the other kids. They weren't in the hall, either.

"Good morning, Dawn," he said. "Go ahead and take your seat."

"But where is everybody?" Dawn asked.

At first she was elated—*no sign of Leah!*—but then that quickly morphed into worry. But before Mr. Blankenship could answer, the bell sounded.

As if on cue, Phillipa rushed in, red-faced and gushing apologies.

"Samson ran away into the woods!" she huffed and puffed. "I had to go fetch him."

"Always Samson, huh?" Mr. Blankenship said. "Bless that pup's heart."

Phillipa saw the empty classroom. "Uh, why isn't anybody else here?"

"They're still out sick," Mr. Blankenship said.

"What's wrong with them?" Phillipa asked, exchanging worried looks with Dawn.

"Well, we're not sure," Mr. Blankenship said. "It's kind of a mystery."

"What do you mean?" Dawn asked, swallowing hard.

"Apparently, they can't stay awake," Mr. Blankenship said. "Guess they've been sleeping since we sent them home yesterday."

"Sleeping?" Dawn repeated.

He nodded. "Yes, the nurse suspects it's a virus making them tired. Most likely, they'll feel better soon. But I'll keep you posted."

"Thanks, Mr. Blankenship," Phillipa said. Then she caught Dawn's eye. "Wow, I'm glad I skipped the party. That's so strange. I wonder what happened."

"Uh, yeah," Dawn said, feeling sick to her stomach.

Nervously, she began to remember her deal with the fairy about the spinning wheel.

As Mr. Blankenship began teaching, Dawn did her best to focus on the positive things happening, like the possibility of her getting to go home and the spinning wheel's saving her aunts' shop. Still, she had a bad feeling.

And she couldn't seem to shake it.

* * *

"Wow, it really does look like a castle," Dawn said, peering up at Phillipa's house as she stepped off her bike.

Her aunts had granted her the whole afternoon off to go over to Phillipa's house.

Dawn took in the house, located on the edge of town by the forest. The Forbidden Mountains loomed over it, casting the place into shadow. Dawn thought Phillipa had been making a joke when she said it looked like a castle, but it actually resembled the castles from Mr. Blankenship's history lesson. It was made out of gray stone and even had a mini moat encircling it with a drawbridge and two towers.

"How big is it?" Dawn asked.

"It's humongous, but it's drafty and gets cold in the winter," Phillipa said. "My bedroom is in that tower."

Phillipa pointed to the tallest one—a spire that steepled up to the sky. It had arched stained glass windows that depicted a prince riding a white horse, brandishing a broadsword. Rose vines climbed up the stone tower, blooming their crimson blossoms. But Dawn could see the thorns jabbing out like needles underneath the leaves.

"Whoa . . ." Dawn said in awe. "So you're like the *real* princess around here."

"At your service," Phillipa said with a bow. "Or maybe more like a prince. I don't like dresses very much."

She pointed to her dusty coveralls and boots. They both laughed.

"How'd you get a castle for a house?" Dawn said. "I didn't know they had them here."

"Oh, my great-grandfather built it when my ancestors came over from England. In fact, they founded the whole town. That's also why it's named . . ."

"Castletown," Dawn finished. "That makes total sense—"

Woof! Woof!

A giant white dog barked and charged toward them.

The huge ball of fluff barreled into Phillipa, almost knocking her over in his desperation to lick her face.

"Down, boy!" Phillipa giggled between licks.

Dawn guessed there were horses smaller than the dog. He had a fluffy white coat and an adorable face.

"So, this is the famous Samson," Dawn quipped. "Eater of homework. Escaper into the woods. Licker of faces."

"Yup, the one and only," Phillipa said with a snort. "He's a Great Pyrenees. They're bred to protect sheep, but mostly he eats and sleeps."

"Ha, he looks harmless," Dawn said. "But apparently, if you're a fraction, watch out."

Samson barked in agreement.

"Say hi to my friend," Phillipa said, petting his fluffy head. "That's Dawn."

"*Woof!*" Samson barked and trotted over. Dawn worried that he'd knock her over with licks, too. But instead, he sat like a good boy and held out his paw.

"Uh, hi there," Dawn said, reaching out and shaking the dog's paw. "Pleased to meet you."

"Hey, I'll race ya!" Phillipa said.

With that, they mounted their bikes and took off toward the woods. Samson chased after them. They skirted the edge of the forest. A cold wind stirred up and hit Dawn's face. The leaves rattled like dry rain.

Phillipa skidded to a halt. Dawn joined her. "Beat ya!" Phillipa said.

"Well, my bike is like older than both our ages combined," Dawn said with an eye roll.

"Truth," Phillipa agreed.

Dawn peered into the thick woods. The mountains rose over them, looking purple in the fading afternoon sunlight. Their snowcapped peaks glistened like diamonds.

"Why do I get such a bad feeling about that forest?" Dawn asked, as another gust of wind billowed out and shook the trees.

Phillipa followed her gaze. "Well, you always gotta be careful out there. That's why we stay on the edge of the forest. We don't venture in there much, even for hunting season."

"Really?" Dawn said. "What are you afraid of?"

"The usual suspects," Phillipa said. "Wild animals,

like bears and feral pigs. I know pigs don't sound scary . . . but they're super dangerous. Deadly, even. But there's more."

"More than killer pigs?" Dawn asked. She tried to picture a killer pig, but all she could think of was a goofy pink animal, like Wilbur from *Charlotte's Web*.

Phillipa hesitated. "Uh, just some stupid stories. About the forest and the Forbidden Mountains," she said.

"Forbidden Mountains?" Dawn asked, swallowing hard. "Why do they call them that?"

"Why do ya think?" Phillipa said. "Cuz they do look kind of *forbidden*, don't they? They have snow on their peaks year-round. Even in the summer."

"That's strange," Dawn asked. "Is that all?"

"Well, there have always been rumors of magic that hides in the forest," Phillipa said. "But I think they're just spooky stories made up to scare kids and keep them out of the woods so they don't run off and encounter killer pigs, or other dangerous creatures."

"Like Samson?" Dawn said, patting his head.

"Exactly!" Phillipa laughed. "Boo!"

She jumped at Dawn, who leapt back in fear; then

they both broke into peals of laughter. Despite the eerie feeling she got from the forest, Dawn was starting to feel at ease.

* * *

"Hey, I should get home for dinner," Phillipa said. They'd been biking around the forest for the last few hours. "See you tomorrow?"

"Yup, bright and early," Dawn said, turning her bike around toward her aunts' cottage. It lay a short ride away on the other side of the forest.

The wind whipped up again, blowing down from the snowy mountains and hitting her. It was frigid and froze Dawn to the bones.

Dawn shivered and pedaled faster. Black clouds began to swirl overhead. Lightning flashed, followed by a sharp clap of thunder that shook the ground. This storm seemed to come out of nowhere.

Dawn had a bad feeling. She skirted the woods, staying out of reach of the trees.

More lightning flashed, and thunder boomed. Rain started pelting her and making it hard to see.

Then, suddenly—

Caw! Caw!

A swarm of ravens burst from the trees and flew at her. Dawn ducked down and tried to avoid them, but her bike wobbled.

One raven dive-bombed her, barely missing her head. Was it the one from the shed?

Then, over the cacophony of raven cries, another sound reached her ears.

It was a hideous cackle.

It sounded just like the dark fairy. The storm kicked up even more, almost blowing Dawn off the bike. The lead raven circled back, took aim—and flew at her again.

And this time its trajectory was dead-on.

"No!" Dawn screamed, trying to pedal away. She raised her hands to protect her face.

But the raven dove at her, a familiar menacing voice echoing out of its beak.

"Poor simple fool!"

11
SLEEPING SICKNESS

"**N**o, get away!"

The ravens circled and flew at Dawn like a black cloud—wings flapping, beaks open and cawing as they stared at her with beady dark pupils.

Dawn pedaled faster as sweat dripped down her brow, mixing with the cold rain. Lightning lit up the dark skies, and thunder rumbled.

Up ahead, she spotted her aunts' cottage. She zoomed up the gravel driveway, then threw her bike down and burst inside the front door.

Slam!

She shut the door behind her, barely escaping their

talons. She was panting, red-faced, and sweating from head to toe.

"Dearie, what's wrong?" Aunt Fleur said, rushing over to her.

"Did something happen on your way home?" Aunt Merry added.

"Uh, I got caught in that thunderstorm," Dawn said breathlessly. "It came out of nowhere! And these ravens attacked me. Be careful—they might still be outside."

Her aunts gave her a weird look, then peered through the window in the front door.

Aunt Merry frowned. "What storm?"

"Dearie, I don't see any ravens out there," Aunt Fleur said. "Sure you saw them?"

Dawn followed their gazes; then her mouth dropped open in shock.

The skies were blue and crystal clear.

There wasn't a cloud in sight. There was certainly no lightning or thunder or rain. Stranger yet, there were no ravens outside, either. Her bike lay there, discarded in the gravel driveway.

Feeling unsettled, Dawn looked down at her clothes.

They weren't wet, even though rain had pelted her the whole way home. Likewise, the ground outside was dry, and so was her bike.

"Really, I swear . . . th-they were right there," Dawn stammered. "A whole pack of them."

"You mean an unkindness?" Aunt Fleur said, scanning the clear skies.

"A what?" Dawn asked.

"A group of ravens is called an unkindness," Aunt Merry said. "In the old days, some folks thought they were harbingers of ill-fortune, or even death."

"But those are just silly old fairy tales," Aunt Fleur said quickly. "Stop scaring the poor child. She's already had quite a fright."

But that gave Dawn a chill.

An unkindness.

She didn't like the sound of that at all.

"You have to believe me!" Dawn said. "I was biking home by the forest, and this storm just came out of nowhere. Then, the birds started attacking me."

Both aunts watched her with worried eyes. Aunt Fleur reached out and felt her forehead.

"Are you feeling okay, dearie?" Aunt Fleur said. "We heard about that sickness going around school. The nurse phoned us."

"Let me fetch you a spot of tea," Aunt Merry said. "I was fixin' to brew some up anyway."

"I swear it's true," Dawn said, but now even she felt like she had been imagining things. She scanned the skies one last time, but that didn't change anything.

"Come, child, lie down," Aunt Fleur said, leading Dawn up the stairs to her bedroom.

"There, there . . . just rest now," her aunt said. "Tomorrow is a big day! The auction house plans to sell off the spinning wheel."

"Oh, that's so exciting," Dawn said weakly.

As she crawled into bed, she felt completely freaked out. She knew what she had seen.

She remembered Maleficent and her own promise to return the spinning wheel in exchange for Maleficent's punishing Leah and her friends. But that had just been her imagination, right? None of that was real.

It couldn't be.

* * *

SLEEPING SICKNESS

The next day at school, Dawn walked into a noisy, full classroom. She smiled at the sight of all the kids swarming around their desks. Her worries about having somehow caused the sleeping sickness instantly evaporated.

"Can you believe that sickness?" the boy who had teased her on her first day said to his friend.

"OMG, I was so sleepy!" the girl replied, miming an exaggerated yawn.

"Yup, all I did was pass out in bed," the boy said. "It must've been from Leah's party."

"Think it was the flu?" the girl said. "Or something else?"

"Who knows?" the boy said. "At least we're all better."

Everyone was chattering and seemed energetic and fully recovered . . . except for one.

Leah's desk remained empty.

Dawn felt a jolt of fear but forced it back.

The bell rang, and she half expected Leah to rush in, but only Mr. Blankenship strode through the door.

"*Psssst* . . . where's Leah?" Dawn said, sliding into her spot next to Phillipa.

They both peered at the empty desk.

"My pops talked to her folks," Phillipa whispered. "Apparently, she just keeps sleeping and can't wake up."

"But all the other kids are better," Dawn said.

Even though it was smaller than her old school, after two days of just her and Phillipa in class, it felt packed to the brim.

"Guess whatever it was hit her the hardest," Phillipa said with a frown. "She probably just needs to sleep it off."

"Let's hope so," Dawn said.

She regretted wishing ill upon Leah. At first, her absence from school had been a fun reprieve, plus the payback felt nice after her cruel prank. But now reality had set in. Dawn didn't actually want Leah to be sick.

She'll be better soon, Dawn reassured herself. All the other kids were better, right?

Plus, that day ended up being the best day at school yet. Without Leah around to tease her, the other students warmed up to Dawn. Several kids actually sat with her and Phillipa at lunch, including a boy named Fred and his friend Winnie. She had curly brown hair that bounced around as she talked. "That seat taken?"

"Sit your behind down already," Phillipa said.

Both their names sounded strange and old-fashioned to Dawn, but that was true for so many things in Castletown. Often, it reminded her of a time capsule, frozen and unchanging, while the rest of the world barreled forward into the future.

They dug into their school lunches—something called chicken-fried steak, which Dawn had never heard of. It was served over mashed potatoes with a weird white gravy.

"Well, is it *chicken* or *steak*?" Dawn asked, spearing a piece and inspecting it closer.

Everybody laughed at her confusion.

"Bless your heart! You've never had it before?" Winnie said. "My mama cooks it up on the regular."

"Yeah, what did y'all eat up north?" Fred asked.

"Not this," Dawn said, frowning at the meat on her tray. "What animal does it come from?"

"It's cow," Winnie said.

"Then why's it called chicken?" Dawn asked, still totally confused. She tried a tiny bite. To her surprise, it actually tasted quite yummy.

"'Cuz they fry it up like chicken," Fred said, chuckling. "They *chicken fry* it. Make sense?"

"Y'all are weird," Dawn said, trying out the new word. "But this is kind of tasty."

They all beamed at her. And then something shocking happened. Stephanie and Kaylee approached their table, clutching their trays. They seemed nervous.

"Uh, hey there," Stephanie said.

"What do y'all want?" Phillipa said, giving them a look that said, *Don't mess with my friend.*

"Look, we're sorry about the prank," Kaylee said. "It got out of hand."

"And for lying and getting you into trouble," Stephanie added. "Leah made us do it. But we want you to forgive us."

Dawn couldn't believe her ears. "What made you change your mind?" she asked them.

"Being home sick," Kaylee said. "The whole time I was sleeping, I had these terrible nightmares. This fairy kept haunting me."

"Yeah, me too," Stephanie said. "It's so weird. This voice said we were being punished for lying about you."

They both peered at her. Dawn stopped chewing.

Suddenly, she couldn't breathe.

"Here, drink water," Phillipa said, handing her a bottle and pounding on her back.

Dawn drank thirstily. Once she got ahold of herself, she found her voice. It sounded raspy. "Did you find out the fairy's name?" she asked. "What did she look like?"

An awkward moment of silence passed.

"Look, it's just a weird dream," Kaylee said. "We probably watched the same scary movie or something, and it caused the dreams."

"Yeah, it can't be real," Stephanie said. "Nobody has the *same* dreams."

"Is that all you remember?" Dawn asked.

Kaylee cocked her eyebrow. "Why're you so interested?"

"Dunno, just curious," Dawn said, trying to sound casual, though her heart was pounding.

"Hmm . . . there was one more thing," Stephanie said, searching her memory. "But it's kind of strange. The fairy said she wanted something back. That a girl broke her deal and stole it from her."

"What did she want?" Dawn asked, though she already guessed the answer.

Stephanie grimaced and shut her eyes.

"A spinning wheel."

Suddenly, the whole table except for Dawn burst out laughing.

"A fairy wants a spinning wheel?" Fred laughed. "That's a new one. Never heard that joke before."

"Seriously, y'all got crazy imaginations," Phillipa said, chuckling along. "A spinning wheel, of all things!"

"Well, Ma does like to sew," Stephanie said. "She's even got a whole room set up for it."

"You should invite the fairy over," Phillipa joked. "Maybe we can have a sewing circle with her. Just avoid the dark fairies. They can totally curse you."

That prompted more laughter.

Dawn tried to join them, but her laugh came out sounding weak. She didn't want them to know the truth—that inside, she was terrified.

The sleeping sickness, the nightmares, the dark fairy, the spinning wheel, their shared dreams—none of that could be a coincidence.

That meant Maleficent was real.

And the sickness wasn't any ordinary sickness—it was a curse.

12

SNORE YOU LATER

"**R**ace ya to the corner store!" Phillipa called after school, then took off on her bike.

Dawn hesitated, unsure if she should go.

The dark fairy wanted her spinning wheel back.

The strange coincidence of Kaylee and Stephanie having the same dream unsettled her. She remembered the deal she'd made with Maleficent to punish Leah for excluding her from the birthday party. The dark fairy must have unleashed the sleeping curse on the kids. Even though it sounded far-fetched, it was the only explanation for everything that had happened.

But what could Dawn do about it?

All the other kids were better already, and Leah was

sure to wake up and come around any day now. The curse seemed to have a time limit and wear off, based on the kids' making full recoveries. Plus, the wheel was about to get auctioned off. Her aunts needed to sell it to save their shop. Worse yet, the spinning wheel was locked up in a safe.

How would she get it out?

But there was more to her reluctance. She had a bad feeling about returning the wheel. What would the fairy do if she actually got it back?

Dawn remembered Maleficent saying something about how the wheel had been stolen long before and how losing it had weakened her powers. What if the dark fairy got stronger?

So then, wasn't it better if it got sold off to a buyer far away?

"You're on," Dawn called back, having come to a decision. There was nothing she could do about the fairy and the wheel. "And no fair, you got a head start," she added.

She chased after Phillipa, who had raced ahead. Dawn's bike wobbled and squeaked. Luckily, the corner store was on the way to Spindles 'N' Things.

Dawn caught up to Phillipa as they both careered into the town center.

They squealed to a stop at the corner drugstore, Castletown Pharmacy. Dawn swallowed hard as her eyes fell on the cheerful red awning with a castle logo. She remembered how she had gotten caught shoplifting at a place like this back in the big city. Well, not shoplifting . . . but helping those who were.

Criminal.

The taunt echoed through her head, but she pushed back against it. *Not anymore,* she thought, *I've changed. . . . I would never do that again or break any laws.*

"Candy time?" Phillipa said. "Hey, Earth to Dawn. Come in, are you there?"

That snapped her out of her thoughts. Dawn forced a smile.

"Chocolate, yes please!"

They placed their bikes in the rack on the sidewalk (no need for locks), then headed into the shop. The door let out a cheerful ring as they entered. The store was small and a bit old-fashioned, but it sported modern medicines and brands. A handful of other shoppers browsed the aisles, selecting items from the well-stocked shelves and placing them in their shopping baskets. They looked over as the two girls trotted into the store and grabbed candy.

Dawn felt their eyes on her. She had that familiar dread that they'd find out about her past or, worse, that they already knew what she'd done to get sent away.

Everyone in Castletown knew each other, so if they didn't recognize someone, that turned heads your way as well.

The kindly shopkeeper—an older man with thinning hair—greeted them.

"Howdy, ladies," Mr. Crowley called out. "How can I help you?"

"Candy," Phillipa said. "We need some *stat*. Also, my pops says to tell you hello. And refill his meds. He'll stop by after work."

"Will do. And holler back at him, will ya?" Mr. Crowley said, then busied himself behind the checkout counter. "Tell him we're overdue for a fishing trip."

"Yes, sir," Phillipa said. "Pops loves getting out on that lake."

"Sure does," Mr. Crowley said. "Not that he ever

catches anything. At least, not that's edible." He let out a chuckle, then turned to Dawn. "Oh, and who's your friend here?"

"I'm Dawn," she replied. "Nice to meet you! I moved in with my aunts down the road. Merry and Fleur?"

The shopkeeper started to rub his eyes and yawn. "Oh, dear, pardon me. What was that?" he said in a sleepy voice.

"Merry and Fleur?" Dawn tried again. "I'm living with my aunts. . . ."

His eyelids drooped; then he started awake. "Your aunts? Those old gals?"

"Yeah, I'm here for the rest of the semester . . ."

But then Dawn trailed off. The shopkeeper tipped his head forward, leaning onto the counter . . . and started snoring loudly. He was fast asleep.

"Mr. Crowley?" Phillipa said. She leaned over and nudged his shoulder.

He startled and gasped. "Oh, my, where am I? What's happening?"

"Uh, you're at work," Phillipa said. "You fell asleep."

"Oh dear, so sorry," he said. "I don't know what's gotten into me."

His eyes shifted to Dawn. He blinked at her without any hint of recognition.

"Oh, and who's your friend here?"

"I'm Dawn," she repeated herself. "I moved in with . . ."

Before she could finish, the shopkeeper dozed off on his feet. His chin rested on his chest. Dawn swept her gaze around the store, seeing the other customers clutching wire shopping baskets and looking at them with curious expressions. She made eye contact with each of them, before turning back to the snoring shopkeeper.

"Uh, Mr. Crowley?" Phillipa prodded him awake . . . again.

He blinked at Phillipa, then looked at Dawn with a puzzled expression. "Oh, sorry about that. What were you saying? Dear, who is your new friend here?"

Again, he'd completely forgotten who Dawn was. It was like a loop. Dawn tried to answer him again, and again he fell asleep on his feet, snoring away.

A chill crept up her spine, freezing her. Suddenly, Dawn heard more snoring coming from behind them. *Oh, no,* she thought.

Slowly, Dawn turned and gazed around the pharmacy. Every customer in there had dozed off—on their feet. Snores echoed throughout the shop, as the customers slept upright, still clutching their shopping baskets and bags.

"What the heck?" Phillipa said. "Wow, think they caught the virus, too?"

But Dawn was already backing away from her friend. She had a feeling that she knew what was causing this— and it wasn't a virus.

It was her.

It was the sleeping curse from the dark fairy. Not only that, but clearly it was growing stronger. She had to get out of there—before she got her friend sick, too.

"Uh, sorry . . . I-I'm late for work," Dawn stammered, backing away. She looked down to avoid making eye contact with Phillipa. "I've gotta go."

"Hey, wait . . ." Phillipa called after her.

But Dawn was already out the door before Phillipa could finish. She grabbed her bike and looked back into the shop. Slowly, one by one, the shoppers woke up from their unintentional naps. They returned to browsing, as if nothing had happened.

Meanwhile, it took Mr. Crowley the longest to come around. Phillipa nudged him a few times, and Dawn found herself worried he'd never wake up. But finally he startled to attention, looking bewildered.

He quickly turned back to normal, interacting with Phillipa and checking out the other shoppers. But Dawn felt sick to her stomach. It seemed that everyone she made eye contact with fell asleep. It didn't matter where they were or what they were doing.

Dawn pedaled as fast as she could toward the antique shop. She kept her eyes down, focused on the pavement in front of her. If drivers coming in contact with her fell asleep while on the road . . . well . . . she didn't even want to think about that.

One question tormented her: how was she going to make it stop?

13
POOR SIMPLE FOOL

"**I** have to get the spinning wheel back," Dawn whispered to herself.

That was the only solution.

What had just happened in the corner store freaked her out.

She couldn't stop thinking about the way those strangers had fallen asleep on their feet, snoring and oblivious to the world around them. The curse was definitely growing stronger. And it would surely keep infecting people unless she followed through on her promise to the fairy. Dawn couldn't worry anymore about the consequences of giving it back. The curse was ruining her life, and now everyone around her was in danger.

Dawn skidded up to the antique shop and threw her bike down under the awning. Then, she burst through the front doors, preparing to come clean to her aunts and beg them to give her the wheel so she could return it to the fairy. They'd simply have to find another way to save the shop.

On her way toward the counter, Dawn swiped a pair of old cat's-eye sunglasses off the rack to shield her eyes. She didn't want to infect her aunts with the sleeping curse.

It was important to keep them safe.

The phone rang. "Spindles 'N' Things."

Dawn could hear Aunt Merry's cheerful voice echoing through the shop, as she passed down the packed aisles.

"Oh dear, you found a buyer!" Aunt Merry exclaimed, sounding super excited. "The auction was a success? A *big* success? How much . . ."

Dawn heard hushed voices, then the *clack* as Merry hung up the receiver.

"Fleur, they sold the spinning wheel!" she called out. "It's enough to save our shop . . . and get the bank off our backs. This is the biggest blessing."

"Oh, my, that is good news indeed," Aunt Fleur chirped.

"The buyer's coming by the shop Monday afternoon to collect the wheel," Aunt Merry went on. "But the auction house is wiring us the money right away."

Dawn felt a jolt of fear. If they already sold the spinning wheel, then how could she get it back now? And the money was on the way? Worse yet, the buyer was coming in three short days to retrieve it. Her stomach sank as she thought about it.

"Can you believe it?" Merry said. "Oh, Fleur . . . we're saved! And it's all thanks to Dawn. We should get her a nice present with the money as a thank-you."

"Lovely idea," Fleur said. "What should we get her?"

"Maybe a plane ticket to visit her parents and friends back in the city?" Merry suggested. "You know, she's been adjusting well overall. But I know she's still homesick."

"What a great plan!" Fleur agreed.

This only made Dawn feel *worse*. Her stomach dropped again.

Here her aunts were planning to get her the best gift in the whole world, a way for her to visit her true home, and she'd brought a terrible curse upon them by making a deal with a dark fairy. This was even worse than when she got caught helping shoplifters.

"Oh, but let's keep the spinning wheel locked up in the safe," Fleur said. "We can't risk anyone trying to steal it."

"Oh yes, it's far too valuable," Merry agreed.

Dawn swallowed hard against the churning in her stomach. A thousand terrible scenarios rushed through her head, each worse than the last. She needed to think of a plan—fast.

Dawn slipped out of the aisles and called out to her aunts. She needed somewhere private to gather her thoughts. "Uh, I'm going to clean out the shed some more. . . ."

"My dear, what on earth are you wearing?" Merry said with a chuckle.

"Let me see those," Fleur said, swiping the sunglasses from Dawn's face before she could protest. "Are those sunglasses from our shop?"

But as soon as they looked into Dawn's eyes, they nodded off and fell fast asleep. Their chins rested on their chests, which rose and fell in easy rhythm with their deep breathing. Aunt Fleur still held the sunglasses in her hand. Their snoring echoed through the shop.

With a deep shiver, Dawn backed up slowly.

Oh, no . . .

Dawn took the glasses and left Aunt Merry and Aunt Fleur snoring away behind the register. She slipped out of the shop and into the shed, hoping they'd wake with her gone.

The dark fairy's curse was clearly growing stronger and haunting her. All Dawn had wanted was revenge on Leah for not inviting her to the party. But now everything was backfiring.

It was even affecting her aunts.

Would Phillipa be next?

I need to get the spinning wheel.

But it was locked up in the safe at the office.

Dawn put the sunglasses back on and poked around the shed as she tried to calm down.

She was completely alone. Feeling despondent, she nudged a pile of junk with her foot. The old sword toppled over with a loud clang.

She pulled it out of the sheath and ran her finger along the blade.

"Ouch!" she cried as it sliced right through her skin. Blood dripped down her finger and splattered on the ground. How was it so sharp?

Uneasily, Dawn slid the sword back into the sheath and set it down.

Suddenly—

Caw! Caw!

A raven took off from the rafters and began circling above her. Dawn ducked but then relaxed.

As it settled back down, she proceeded deeper, toward the back of the shed. The light from the windows didn't reach this far back; the space was cast in shadow.

All the way in the back, something large was covered by a tarp. What was it?

Dawn reached out and pulled the covering off—*swish*. It slid to the ground, releasing a puff of dust and revealing an antique gilded standing mirror. The frame rocked forward, catching the light with a green flash.

Caw! Caw!

The raven took off again, fluttering around the rafters.

Dawn started back.

But then, the mirror slumped forward and the flash of green light was gone.

Just a play of light and shadow, she decided. Nothing to be afraid of. She was just jumpy from everything. Plus, she was wearing the dark sunglasses. It was easy to think she was seeing things.

Dawn removed the glasses, then pushed the mirror back. The glass was tarnished and bent. Her features looked elongated and distorted.

I'm a monster, she thought. *This is all my fault.*

Why did trouble seem to follow her like a curse? Even being sent thousands of miles away changed nothing. If anything, it had gotten worse.

She peered at her distorted face in the mirror.

Suddenly—

Her reflection morphed into a dark shadow, growing horns and glowing yellow eyes. Another raven took off, circling and cawing. It then dove at her.

Dawn jumped away, barely avoiding the bird's sharp talons. Then the horned shadow grew taller in the mirror, raising a staff with a crystal orb on it. It now towered over Dawn.

"Criminal!" the shadow shrieked.

"Wh-what?"

"Rabble!" it whispered fiercely. "We had a deal! Where's my spinning wheel?"

Dawn cowered from the mirror. "I'm sorry . . . I didn't mean it!"

She cried out, as the mirror rocked forward again with a flash of emerald light. She tipped the mirror, then cringed back, bracing herself. . . .

But it was back to being just an ordinary mirror.

All it showed was Dawn's warped reflection staring back at her. Even the raven had settled down again and was no longer attacking her.

But Maleficent was clearly angry. This would keep happening unless she honored their deal. But the spinning wheel had been sold off, and worse, the buyer was coming to the shop on Monday afternoon.

What was Dawn going to do?

14
EVERY ROSE
HAS A THORN

The weekend passed in a blur. Dawn was awakened each night by terrible nightmares of ravens attacking her and that horrible voice calling her *criminal*.

She hid out in her bedroom or wore the vintage sunglasses everywhere she went, even inside the house, hoping to protect her aunts. Her aunts no longer rose early in the morning but slept later and later each day. And when they woke, they were tired and not their usual cheerful selves.

So on Sunday, Dawn crept out of the house to get as far away from them as possible. Wearing the sunglasses, she wandered through the walled garden, taking in the fresh roses. She ran her fingers along the soft petals, then smelled them . . . and . . . sneezed, of course.

"Hey there, stranger!"

A voice echoed out, surprising her. Dawn spun around.

Woof!

Samson clomped up to her with his big tongue flopping. Phillipa sat on her bike. Dawn relaxed, though fear still curdled in her stomach. She felt . . . well . . . cursed.

But she was also grateful for the company.

"Uh, what's with those weird old glasses?" Phillipa asked, scrunching up her nose.

Dawn was afraid that if she took them off, Phillipa would fall asleep. "They're from the shop. I thought I'd try out a new look. Something more . . . uh . . . vintage."

"Vintage?"

"What, you don't like it?" Dawn asked.

"It's not that," Phillipa said. "More like it doesn't really go with your look. All those hip city clothes." She motioned at Dawn's designer jeans, new sneakers, and black top with cutouts.

"Ugh, I know," Dawn said. "But I can't take them off."

"Why not?" Phillipa said with a frown. "It's not even that bright out today."

Dawn braced herself, then confessed.

"*'Cuz* . . . if I do . . . then you'll fall asleep," she said quickly. "Like what happened to that shopkeeper in the corner store."

"That has ya worried?" Phillipa said with a snort-laugh. "Mr. Crowley is always dozing off like that. When we go over to his farm so Pops can watch the Braves games, he always passes out. He even calls baseball his nap time."

"Look, I'm serious," Dawn said, feeling the heavy glasses perched on her nose. "You won't be able to stay awake if you look in my eyes."

A cold wind stirred up in the forest and whisked their way, making Dawn shiver. She wrapped her arms around her chest to kindle some warmth.

"Listen, I won't fall asleep," Phillipa said. "Try me! I had a good night's sleep. Though I did have weird dreams about evil fairies and princes and fire-breathing dragons. But it's probably that new fantasy book I snagged at the library. Do it already."

Dawn bit her lip. But she wouldn't take the glasses off.

"I promise, I won't fall asleep," Phillipa said, dragging her hand across her chest. "Cross my heart and hope to die—"

"Ugh, that's what I'm afraid of!" Dawn said. "It's not funny."

Phillipa turned more serious. "Well, we might as well test it out so you can stop acting so weird and we can have some actual fun today. Worst case, you can wake me up, right?"

Before Dawn could protest again, Phillipa swiped the sunglasses from her face. "Samson, keep away!" she said, tossing them to the dog.

He trotted off with his prize, thrilled to have a new toy to carry around and show off to anyone who crossed paths with him. Dawn shut her eyes and held her breath, expecting Phillipa to fall asleep on her feet. She waited for the familiar sound of snoring. But it stayed quiet.

Slowly, she cracked her eyes open.

But . . . nothing happened.

Phillipa stayed wide-awake and alert.

Their eyes met, and Dawn held her gaze just to be sure. She stared in Phillipa's eyes for another long minute. But her friend didn't even so much as yawn.

"See? I'm awake!" Phillipa said.

But Dawn's heart still beat faster than normal. So far Phillipa was the only person who seemed immune to the sleeping curse. But would it last?

Dawn pushed that thought away and forced a smile.

"So, why'd you come over?" she asked. "I wasn't expecting you."

"Well, you did rush out of the shop the other day," Phillipa said. "Guess I was worried. Now you're freaking out about me falling asleep. Everything okay?"

"Yeah, I've just been missing home and my friends," Dawn said. She hadn't texted Ronnie and Daniella in the last few days. Now she was the *bad* friend.

It wasn't a lie exactly . . . more like an exaggeration. But she still couldn't tell Phillipa the truth.

I made a deal with a dark fairy, and she put a sleeping curse on me so that everyone I look at falls asleep.

Anyone would think she wasn't making any sense, and Dawn couldn't exactly blame them. Phillipa narrowed her eyes. Dawn knew she could tell that wasn't the *whole* truth.

Not even close.

But Phillipa let it go, instead turning toward the rose garden.

"Wow, I heard there was a maze here," she said, gazing at the towering hedges peppered with red rose blossoms. The entrance was an arched trellis. "Must be super fun!"

"It's not that fun," Dawn said, feeling naked without the sunglasses. She'd been wearing them nonstop for the last few days. "And it's really easy to get lost in. My first day, my aunts had to come and rescue me."

Phillipa laughed. "I still think it sounds awesome. I bet with my help, we could find our way. Plus, Samson always knows the way home. He can lead us out, right?"

Despite her friend's company, Dawn felt anxious and afraid. A chilly wind whipped out again, but this time it came whistling out of the maze. It gave Dawn a bad feeling, but then . . .

"Tag, you're it!" Phillipa said, tapping her shoulder and taking off.

Samson let out a happy bark and plowed after his owner.

"Wait, come back!" Dawn yelled.

But Phillipa vanished into the maze with Samson (and her sunglasses) in tow. Even though she hated the maze, she couldn't let her friend go back in there alone.

With great trepidation, Dawn passed under the archway. She could hear Phillipa's spirited giggles and Samson's barking coming from deeper inside the maze.

"Hey, no fair," Dawn called out. "You got a head start. Wait up—"

But the wind stole her voice. And the deeper into the maze she went, the stronger it grew. There was a flash and a crack. Storm clouds began to swirl overhead, but Dawn tried to ignore them.

The maze became darker and colder as she wound her way between the hedges, circling further into the labyrinth. She shivered.

Suddenly, ravens swarmed in the sky, blacking out the sun.

Caw! Caw!

She didn't hear Phillipa or Samson anymore.

That worried her.

"Phillipa, come on!" Dawn said. "Stop goofing around and playing tricks on me. There's a big storm coming! Let's go—"

Lightning pulsed, then thunder rumbled and shook the ground. Rain quickly soaked Dawn. She hurried under an archway for shelter. The rain pummeled her anyway. It was cold, and she shivered uncontrollably.

"It's not funny anymore," she called to Phillipa. "Please, let's go back!"

But then, something pricked her skin.

No, more like . . . *stabbed* it.

Dawn spun around right as the rose vines shot out and grabbed her. They wrapped around her body, pulling her into the thick hedges. She cried out in pain, trying to wrench herself free. But they held her tight.

"No, let me go!" she screamed.

They bound her wrists behind her, cutting off the circulation as they pulled her further into the hedge. Razor-sharp thorns poked out of the brush, ready to slice through her skin.

Maybe even slit her throat.

Dawn struggled harder, but the vines just constricted in response. She felt something wrap around her neck. The end of a vine was in front of her face, positioned as if it was staring right at her. Then, without warning, it snaked down her throat, just like in her horrible nightmare.

She couldn't breathe or even scream, as the vine filled up her mouth. It slithered down her throat, wriggling inside her.

Lightning flashed and thunder rang out around her. And then, as if carried by the wind, an unnatural cackle echoed through the maze.

"You're a disgrace to the forces of evil!"

15
FORCES OF EVIL

"**H**old on, I'm getting you out!"

Dimly, Dawn heard a voice. Thorns dug into her flesh—but then, miraculously, the vines released her. She felt them slide out of her mouth. Finally, she was able to breathe. . . .

She gasped for air, falling to her knees and panting.

"Whoa, what happened?" Phillipa said. "You were stuck in that big ole hedge. Listen, just focus on breathing."

Samson licked her face again, trying to revive her. "Good boy," Dawn rasped through her scratchy throat, patting his head in thanks. Dog licks had healing powers, she decided.

"I don't know . . . what happened," Dawn said. "That storm came out of nowhere . . . and then . . . the maze . . . attacked me."

Phillipa now looked even more worried.

"What storm?"

Dawn looked up. Just like the other day when the ravens had chased her, the skies were clear and sunny. There was no storm. She glanced at the hedge that had attacked her, but it looked like an ordinary rosebush now.

"Well, I believe you," Phillipa said. "When I found you, those vines were wrapped around you. Something is definitely going on."

Phillipa walked over and picked up from the ground a vine that had been severed in the struggle.

"Look, I know you're not telling me everything," Phillipa went on. "So spit it out."

"You're right," Dawn confessed, unable to keep the secret anymore. "But it's pretty crazy. I'm not sure you're going to believe me."

"Well, a few minutes ago, I didn't think roses could come alive and attack you, either," Phillipa said. "Those suckers had a pretty good hold on you," she continued. "We had to pull them off. They were even . . . *down your throat*! I can't really explain that. So give it a shot."

"Fine," Dawn said. "But let's get out of here first."

"Agreed," Phillipa said. "But, uh . . . you were right. I'm pretty lost now. Know the way out?"

Dawn shook her head. "I told you!"

Her stomach twisted.

But then, Samson barked and grabbed Phillipa's sleeve in his teeth.

"What is it, boy?" Phillipa asked.

"What's he trying to tell you?" Dawn asked.

Phillipa brightened, as he tugged her more insistently.

"*We* might be lost," Phillipa said, "but Samson knows the way out. Let's go!"

* * *

"So, what's this crazy thing you have to tell me?" Phillipa inquired.

Her words hung thick in the air.

The sun was moving down, signaling that it was late afternoon.

FORCES OF EVIL

Dawn sat next to Phillipa on a stone bench outside the rose garden. It still loomed over them with its towering hedges, however. Samson and his strong nose had rescued them from the maze.

Despite the beauty of the roses, all Dawn could think about were the thorns buried under their inviting petals and their sickly-sweet perfume. *It's like a spell designed to lure you in,* she thought, *like the voice from the spinning wheel.*

"Okay, but you have to promise you won't think I'm making things up," Dawn said. "Like what happened at school, when nobody believed me about Leah."

Phillipa giggled. "Remember, even then I believed you."

"Good point," Dawn agreed, thinking of how Phillipa had had her back when none of the other kids in Castletown did. "But what I tell you stays between us. Like a secret."

"Just tell me already," Phillipa said with a roll of her eyes.

Dawn took a deep breath, then told Phillipa

everything—about finding the spinning wheel in the shed and pricking her finger, the green flames erupting out of it, and the dark fairy offering to help her get revenge on Leah.

"So . . . let me get this straight," Phillipa said, starting to look freaked out. "You made a deal with a dark fairy named Maleficent? And you thought that was . . . a good idea? Wow, like, even in my books that would be a super-bad idea. And they're just fiction. This is real."

"Right, I know it's hard to understand," Dawn said, feeling regret pool in her heart like a deep, dark lake. "I was so upset by what Leah did to me, and then seeing all the posts from her birthday made it worse. Maleficent promised to teach Leah a lesson, in exchange for my returning the spinning wheel to her. But now it's starting to backfire.

"I mean, the first day, when Leah and everyone fell asleep in class and got sent home, was kind of awesome," Dawn said, smiling at the memory. "It felt good to be vindicated."

Phillipa smirked. "Yeah, that was pretty great. Leah acts all nice, but really she's a bully. Even the other kids are scared of her."

"Well, you did try to warn me about her," Dawn said. "But I didn't listen."

Phillipa shrugged. "Leah puts on such a good act that it's hard to see through it."

Dawn smiled but then grew more solemn. "But now Leah's still sick. And the curse is growing stronger. At first it was just our class, but now anyone I talk to, or come into contact with, falls asleep. As soon as I open my mouth, they start snoring away on their feet."

"Like in the drugstore?" Phillipa asked with a frown.

"Yup, exactly," Dawn said with a shudder. "That's why I ran away like that. You see, I was worried about making more people sick. But for some reason, you're the only one not affected by it. So now I'm thinking it's because you're my . . ."

"Friend," Phillipa finished.

"At least . . . you *were* my friend," Dawn said, feeling tears threatening to spill from her eyes. "Before I told you I made a deal with a dark fairy."

Phillipa frowned again. "What do you mean?"

"Well, I'm pretty sure after that confession," Dawn

lamented, "you're not gonna want to be friends anymore."

"Uh, what . . . are you kidding?" Phillipa said. "I'm going to help you."

"Wait . . . you are?" Dawn asked in surprise. "You're not freaked out?"

"I mean, I'm a little freaked out," Phillipa admitted, but then excitement lit up her face. "But this is awesome! I knew magic was real. It's just like in my books."

Woof! Samson barked and trotted over. Grass clung to his white fur, staining it green. He had Dawn's sunglasses in his wet mouth. He nosed them into Dawn's hand.

"How are you excited?" Dawn asked.

"A dark fairy!" Phillipa said. "An evil curse! A spinning wheel that's got magic powers!"

Phillipa started pacing around, barely able to contain herself. "I mean, I grew up hearing the tales about Castletown being haunted," she said, "and strange things happening here, especially in the Dark Forest. That's why I love reading fantasy books so much. Anyway, I always knew the stories were true, but nobody believed me. They said they're just made up to scare kids. So crazy, but I was right!"

"So . . . this is a good thing?" Dawn said, scratching her head in confusion.

"Well, not exactly," Phillipa said. "Now that I think about it more . . . what you did was probably a really bad idea."

"What do you mean?" Dawn asked.

"Based on my books, fairies can trick you," Phillipa explained. "They can't be trusted. And their curses aren't easily broken. Especially . . . dark fairies."

"Yeah, that's what I was worried about," Dawn said, swallowing hard. Tears spilled down her cheeks. She couldn't hold them back this time.

She'd never felt so lost, not even when her parents sent her away. Samson licked her face, smothering her with dog kisses and trying to cheer her up. It helped, but only a little.

"What am I going to do?" Dawn cried. "All I wanted was to teach Leah a lesson. But look where that got me!"

"If the dark fairy is so powerful," Phillipa said, thinking it over, "then why doesn't she just take the spinning wheel back for herself?"

"Because she can't," Dawn explained, thinking back

to that fateful day in the shed and the exchange with Maleficent. "The owner has to give it back to her . . . willingly."

"Right, protection spells," Phillipa said. "Those are all over my books. Have you tried to give it back to her yet? Wouldn't that stop the curse?"

"Maybe," Dawn said. "But my aunts auctioned it off already. It turns out that it's really valuable. The buyer is coming to the shop tomorrow. And even if I wanted to take it, they locked it up in the safe where they keep prized antiques."

"Okay, got it," Phillipa said. "Plus, based on my books . . . giving fairies objects of power is probably a bad idea. Someone hid the wheel and put protection spells on it for a reason."

Dawn didn't like the sound of that. "What do you mean?"

"If her power is tied to the spinning wheel, then it could make her even more powerful," Phillipa said.

"Yeah, that's what I'm worried about," Dawn said. "There must be a reason she wants it so badly. She said losing it weakened her powers."

"That's what I was afraid of," Phillipa agreed. "And dark fairies don't use their powers for good."

Dawn felt the tears start welling from her eyes again. "It's all my fault. I can't give her the wheel. But if I don't, then she won't lift the curse or leave me alone."

Phillipa patted her back. "Look, we can fix this. I'm going to help you."

"But how?" Dawn said between ugly sobs.

"Where did this all start?" Phillipa said.

"At the antique shop." Dawn sniffled, wiping away her tears. Samson let out a concerned whine and licked at her face. "In the shed out back, where I found the spinning wheel."

Phillipa started away, then turned back.

"Well, aren't you coming?"

"Coming?" Dawn sniffled, not budging from the bench. She felt hopeless.

But Phillipa grabbed her arm and tugged her up, while Samson barked his encouragement. She dragged Dawn over to their bikes.

"To Spindles 'N' Things, of course," Phillipa said, hopping on her bike and pointing it toward the gravel driveway. "Maybe there's a clue in that shed that can tell us more about what caused this to happen. Or more importantly, *who* caused it."

That made Dawn feel afraid again. She grabbed her bike. "You mean, the dark fairy?"

Phillipa nodded. *"Maleficent."*

Suddenly, ravens burst out of the forest and swarmed overhead, blacking out the sun for a moment and casting them into shadow.

Caw! Caw!

It was an . . . *unkindness*, Dawn remembered her aunts telling her. Were the birds listening to them? Spying on them for the dark fairy, even?

"But this could be really dangerous," Dawn said, remembering the fairy's condescending tone and all the nightmares and hauntings since then. "Sure you want to help me?"

"Yup, you're my friend," Phillipa said in a firm voice. "Plus, this is the only way we can figure out how to make her stop, right?"

Dawn nodded, pulling on her sunglasses to protect others from her. Then, she pedaled after her friend. She felt a stirring hope, something she hadn't felt in a long time. This was still a terrible situation, and she had no idea how they were going to fix it. But somehow, not having to deal with it alone made it less scary.

Samson loped after them, as always. The ravens followed like a permanent shadow.

Caw! Caw!

Dawn glanced back at Samson, wondering why he wasn't chasing the birds.

Then, she realized . . .

Even he looked afraid.

16
THE MISTRESS
OF ALL EVIL

Dawn thrust open the doors. They rumbled, with light spilling into the dark shed.

Caw! Caw!

Bursting from the rafters, a raven dive-bombed them with a fluttering of feathers. "Watch out!" Dawn called, pulling Phillipa out of the way.

But suddenly—

Samson sprang into protection mode. He woofed and chased the raven away, then returned, panting, to their sides. But his hackles remained raised.

He was worried about them.

"Whoa, killer-raven alert," Phillipa said. "Hanging

out with you is all kinds of dangerous. First mazes that attack you, and now birds. What's next?"

"Told ya," Dawn said. "I think the ravens have something to do with the fairy. Like they work for her . . . or know when she's close . . . or they do her bidding . . ." She trailed off, unsure what it all meant.

"They're bewitched," Phillipa whispered.

"What do you mean?" Dawn asked.

"She's a dark fairy, right?" Phillipa said. "So she probably bewitches the ravens. Some fairies can control all sorts of animals, and even humans sometimes."

"Wow," Dawn said, impressed. "Your fantasy books really taught you a lot, huh?"

"They sure did!" Phillipa pulled out her latest library acquisition from her backpack.

"Book nerds really are the heroes," Dawn said with a smirk.

"You got that right. Knowledge is power. Come on, we don't have any time to waste," Phillipa said, pulling her into the shed. "The more we know, the closer we are to fixing this."

Dust danced in the slants of late-afternoon light leaking inside the dim space.

"Wow, look at all this stuff," Phillipa said, taking it all in.

Despite Dawn's efforts to clean it, the shed was still jam-packed with piles of junk.

"Where'd they get all of it?" Phillipa said, sifting through a heap. She tossed aside an old leather shoe and some moth-eaten dolls.

"They buy it from estate sales," Dawn said. "Or abandoned storage lockers. That sort of thing. Most of it hasn't been touched in eons."

"You can say that again," Phillipa said, crinkling up her nose.

"What're we looking for?" Dawn asked, pulling off her sunglasses and starting on another mound.

Phillipa frowned. "Uh, not exactly sure. But any clues about the spinning wheel and where it came from . . . or who took it and hid it . . . or especially the fairy."

"They don't put that in your books?" Dawn quipped, earning a deserved elbow jab from her friend. They worked their way through the shed but found nothing helpful or even interesting. Dawn sat down in frustration, wiping the dust from her face with her shirt.

"It's hopeless," she said, sniffling. "There's nothing back here but a bunch of old junk—"

Woof! Woof!

Samson barked from deeper in the shed, over by the mirror—the one the fairy had bewitched the other day. Dawn felt a jolt of fear.

"Hey, boy, what is it?" Phillipa called, going to investigate.

"Oh, look back here!" Phillipa called out after getting to Samson. She pushed the mirror aside to reveal that Samson was barking at something hidden *behind* it.

"What . . . is it?" Dawn said, following them cautiously. She kept her eyes on the mirror, but it only showed their warped reflections.

Phillipa stood by a large square covered in a dusty tarp. She slid the tarp off with a whoosh, revealing a medieval tapestry.

It depicted images of a spinning wheel.

Dawn felt her breath catch in her throat. A beautiful blond princess was shown pricking her finger on it, while a menacing-looking fairy with glowing yellow eyes cast a sleeping curse on her.

"This is it. . . . That's the dark fairy," Phillipa said.

Woof! Samson barked.

"If you're Sherlock," Dawn said, patting Samson on the head, "then he's Watson."

Phillipa searched around by the tapestry. "I found an old book!" She plopped down by the mirror and slid the ancient-looking book onto her lap. She blew the dust off the leather-bound cover, revealing a title scripted in golden lettering.

Little Briar Rose

Phillipa flipped to the first page and read, "'In past times there were a king and queen, who said every day, "Oh, if only we had a child!"'"

Phillipa flipped through the book, taking in the old story. Dawn followed along and pointed to the next page.

"Look! It's a spinning wheel," she said.

Phillipa kept reading, then looked up from the book. "It says here the king and queen didn't invite the fairy to their daughter's birthday, so she put an evil curse on the baby."

"Wow, that's like what happened to me," Dawn said, sitting back. Her mind went into a tizzy from this new information. "When Leah didn't invite me to her birthday party, the dark fairy said she understood what I was going through."

"Exactly," Phillipa said, flipping to an illustration on the next page. "Anyway, this fairy is . . . dark fey. Just like I thought. That's bad."

Phillipa pointed to the page. The fearful image showed the fairy with two horns, a black-and-purple robe, and a staff crowned with a crystal orb . . . and she stared out with glowing yellow eyes.

"Whoa, that's the fairy I saw," Dawn said. She swallowed hard at the memory of how Maleficent had materialized out of the spinning wheel. "The one I made the deal with."

"She's actually called the Mistress of All Evil," Phillipa said.

"Did she cast a sleeping curse?" Dawn asked, but Phillipa shook her head as she kept on reading.

"No, it's worse than that," Phillipa said, skimming ahead quickly.

Phillipa gasped. "It wasn't just a sleeping curse—it was a *death* curse."

In the images, the fairy swirled her hand around the orb on her staff, depicting visions of monsters—and a spinning wheel. The last picture showed the princess lying on her deathbed.

Phillipa read the original curse from the book: "'Before the sun sets on her sixteenth birthday, she shall prick her finger on the spindle of a spinning wheel . . . and die!'"

"Did she kill the princess?" Dawn asked, as Phillipa flipped the page. They both read on. Dawn's heart pounded faster with each word. Then, Phillipa let out a sigh of relief.

"No, three good fairies protected her," Phillipa said. "So the spell was transformed into a *sleeping* curse that could only be broken by True Love's Kiss. Eventually, a prince saved her."

She pointed to the page she was on. There, a handsome young brown-haired man could be seen mounted on a magnificent white steed. He was brandishing a double-sided broadsword and battling the dark fairy, who had turned herself into a dragon that breathed emerald fire. The next page showed him throwing the sword at the black dragon—and piercing it through the heart. The caption under the image read *Thou Sword of Truth fly swift and sure. That evil die and good endure!*

Phillipa flipped to the final page of the book. That page showed the prince kissing the sleeping Princess Aurora and finally awakening her, along with the whole castle and town. "'And they lived happily ever after. . . .'"

Phillipa flipped the book shut.

"Except the dark fairy didn't perish," Dawn said, knowing that the story didn't end so easily. "And now she wants her spinning wheel back. But what happens if she gets it?"

"I'm not sure," Phillipa said, tapping the book. "Didn't you say something about her magic being infused into the wheel?"

Dawn nodded sharply. "Yeah, that's what she told me."

Phillipa took that in; then a worried expression

crossed her face. "My best guess is that without the wheel, it's only a sleeping curse. But if Maleficent gets it back . . ."

A cold wind whipped through the doors suddenly, slamming them shut.

Phillipa lowered her voice. "Then it becomes a *death* curse."

That hit Dawn hard. She felt her breath catch in her throat. "You mean if she gets it back," Dawn said, as the wind howled, "everyone affected by Maleficent's curse won't just sleep forever . . . they'll die?"

Phillipa nodded and pointed to the tapestry with the spinning wheel and the princess pricking her finger. "Look, the curse is already spreading to other people. You saw what happened in the corner store? If it gets stronger, then it could spread to the whole town."

"Yeah, and it's possible that it won't just stop with our town," Dawn said.

"Yup," Phillipa said. "It could spread to the rest of the world, even."

Those words hit Dawn like a dagger to the heart. She thought about her parents back in the city and her friends

Ronnie and Daniella. Now everyone she loved was in danger, and it was all thanks to her. This time, it *was* her fault. She had no excuses.

Everything they'd just learned only made their situation seem worse. The fairy was far darker and far more powerful than she'd ever imagined.

"There's no way we can give the spinning wheel back," Dawn said with a shiver. She glanced at the book with the prince battling the black dragon.

"Yeah, that would be bad," Phillipa said, following her gaze to it. She tucked the old book into her backpack.

"So what're we going to do?" Dawn asked. The sunlight was fading fast, and darkness would be descending soon.

"The buyer comes tomorrow?" Phillipa said.

"Yes, in the afternoon," Dawn confirmed. "I heard my aunts talking about it."

"Right, I'll take the book home and study it closer," Phillipa said, hopping to her feet. "We'd better get going before night falls. Dark fairies have more power at night, at least according to my books."

"Do you think the book has information that can help

us?" Dawn asked, feeling uncertainty surge through her. "Like how to break the curse?"

What good was a book against a dark fairy? Especially one called the Mistress of All Evil?

"Books often have answers to many of life's problems," Phillipa said, but then her voice turned darker. "But this is a tough situation. All I know is we have to think of something."

Dawn nodded. "And fast."

* * *

They biked through town on the way home. It was the end of the day, and folks meandered on the sidewalks, chatting and hanging out. Samson ran after them, barking and wagging his tail.

Dawn couldn't stop thinking about the story of Briar Rose and the illustrations in the story. What were she and Phillipa going to do?

As they came to the one stop sign, they squealed to a halt. A station wagon screeched to a stop behind them, and also a tractor. *Of course a tractor,* Dawn thought with a roll of her eyes.

Then, suddenly, the woman in the car next to her made eye contact with Dawn . . .

And dozed off at the wheel.

Dawn wasn't wearing her sunglasses.

But then, before Dawn could put her sunglasses back on to shield her eyes, the old man on the tractor glanced over at her—and suddenly fell asleep. He slumped forward, accidentally shifting into drive. The huge farm vehicle started rolling toward them. The plow attached to the front churned toward Phillipa with its razor-sharp blades.

"Watch out!" Dawn yelled, while Samson barked.

Dawn dropped her sunglasses and pushed Phillipa out of the way, just in time.

The tractor and its deadly blades barely missed shredding Dawn to ribbons. But it ran over her sunglasses—*crunch*—crushing them to smithereens. Then, as Dawn glanced around the town's main block in a panic, all the people on the streets fell asleep on their feet.

It was eerie.

All these people were snoring in place. But then . . . they woke up.

Well, they didn't wake up, exactly, but started shuffling toward Dawn with their eyes closed, like slow-moving zombies. Everyone was swarming toward them with their hands outstretched.

"Wh-what's happening?" Phillipa gasped, backing away in fear.

The old man lunged off the tractor and grabbed Dawn by the shoulders. She could smell the fresh-cut grass wafting off his denim overalls. Dawn tried to pull away, but he held on to her tight with his ironclad grip. His eyes were shut, but his lips moved and he hissed at her.

"You poor simple fools thought you could defeat me!" the old man wheezed in a disdainful female voice. "The Mistress of All Evil?"

It was Maleficent's voice coming out of his mouth.

Dawn let out a terrified scream.

17
BEWITCHED

"**G**et off her!" Phillipa yelled, swiping into the man with her bike.

Samson lunged at him and dragged him off Dawn. But all the people from the street shuffled toward them slowly with their arms outstretched. Despite their sluggish pace, they were relentless, forming a circle around Dawn and Phillipa.

"Come on, let's ride," Phillipa said, tugging Dawn away. "Hurry, pedal fast. They're coming for us!"

That kicked Dawn into action. She stood up on her pedals, then rode as hard as she could. They broke through the zombified townsfolk. They sped out of town, with Samson keeping pace. The people lurched and shuffled after them.

Dawn and Phillipa didn't stop until they reached a deserted stretch of road outside town by the woods. Then, they turned to look behind them.

One by one, the people in town startled awake and looked around in surprise, unsure what had happened to them. But they seemed mostly okay, as they returned to their business.

"Whoa, that was close," Phillipa said. She and Dawn were both breathing hard. Even Samson was panting. Darkness was falling fast. The woods were silent—like they were listening to them. "It's getting worse."

"What do we do now?" Dawn asked.

"Uh, I don't know," Phillipa said, stifling a yawn.

"Oh, no, it's affecting you now?" Dawn said.

"Nah, I'm actually tired," she explained. "Like *normal* tired. Not zombie-sleeping-cursed-by-a-dark-fairy tired. It's been a really long day."

"You can say that again," Dawn said, feeling exhausted, too.

"Uh, just go home and get some rest," Phillipa said.

"It's getting dark, which means danger lurks. I'll see you at school in the morning. I'll think of something, I promise."

"I hope so," Dawn said, feeling fear replacing the tiredness in her body. "The buyer's coming to the shop tomorrow. If they sell the wheel, then it will be too late to stop this."

* * *

Dawn showed up to school the next day feeling sick to her stomach over everything that had happened. She made sure to stop by the antique shop on the way for new sunglasses.

Not only did she not have a plan, but the curse was growing stronger. She left her aunts dozing in their shop, hoping they'd wake up after she left.

She hurried through the halls, keeping her eyes hidden behind the dark glasses. Then she slid behind her desk. Phillipa wasn't there yet.

That worried her.

Ring.

Right at the bell, Phillipa rushed in. "Sorry, Mr.

Blankenship. I slept through my alarm. I don't know what got into me."

"That's okay," Mr. Blankenship said with a wry chuckle. "At least it wasn't Samson causing trouble this time. Please, take your seat. Seems everyone is sleepy lately."

Dawn kept her face hidden as Phillipa slid behind her desk, but glimpsed something out of the corner of her eye.

It was Leah.

"OMG, are you okay?" Kaylee said. "We were so, so worried about you."

"Yeah, what happened?" Stephanie added. "You were out like a whole week."

"Honestly, I don't really remember much," Leah said, clearly loving all the attention. "My parents said I just slept the whole time." She smiled and twirled her hair.

Despite her worries, Dawn felt herself growing angry again. That was it? Just a measly week of sleeping?

Leah looked back and spotted Dawn.

"Ugh, what is she wearing?" Leah said with a deep scowl. "Mr. Blankenship, we aren't allowed to wear sunglasses in class, right? Isn't that in the school dress code?"

Mr. Blankenship looked at Dawn. "Sorry, but you'll have to give me those until after class," he said with a shake of his head. "Leah is right."

Dawn immediately panicked.

"Uh, no . . . I can't take them off . . . it's dangerous."

"They're just sunglasses," Mr. Blankenship said with a frown.

"Ugh, she's lying again," Leah said with a pout. "Can't you see that? She thinks she can break the rules and get away with everything. Mr. Blankenship, it's not fair."

"Dawn, if you don't hand those over right now," Mr. Blankenship said sternly, "then I'll have to send you to the principal's office. The rules are clear."

He strode over to her desk and held out his hand. But Dawn held the glasses to her face, refusing to take them off. "No, I can't. . . . I promise there's a perfectly good reason. . . ."

She trailed off, knowing that nobody here would believe her story about curses and dark fairies. She could feel the whole class watching her.

"Dawn, one last chance," Mr. Blankenship said in a strained voice.

Don't do it, Phillipa mouthed.

But Dawn didn't have a choice. She slid the sunglasses off and kept her eyes shut. She placed them in Mr. Blankenship's hand. How was she going to get through the rest of the day?

But then she heard something.

"She's the worst!" Leah whispered. "Always breaking rules."

Kaylee and Stephanie laughed. "Those glasses are . . . hideous," Kaylee said.

"Yeah, why would she want to keep them?" Stephanie added.

The whole class broke out into jeers and laughter. And before she knew what she was doing, Dawn felt terrible rage rush through her.

"Oh, yeah?" Dawn said. "Is that what you think?"

She turned around—and looked right at Leah.

Leah met her eyes and then suddenly fell asleep at her desk. Her head nodded forward, as her snores reverberated around the room. All the other kids turned to watch.

"Oh, no, wake up!" Kaylee said, shaking Leah. She caught Dawn watching them. Her expression morphed to one of horror. "Wait, did you do this to her? Did you cause this?"

"Yeah, this is your fault!" Stephanie cried out.

But then, as they looked directly at Dawn, both girls fell asleep at their desks. Now the whole class turned to look at her. And suddenly, just like the three girls, they each dozed off.

Even Mr. Blankenship started snoring away on his feet.

"No, I swear," Dawn said, suddenly regretting it, "I didn't mean it."

Suddenly, Phillipa grabbed her arm. "Dawn, come on . . . let's go!"

They jumped up from their desks and tiptoed toward the door. All the kids were snoring away. But then . . . they jerked their heads around, even though their eyes were still closed.

Slowly, like zombies, they rose to their feet. Dawn and Phillipa backed away in fear.

Even Mr. Blankenship lunged toward Phillipa.

"Poor simple fools!" he hissed in the dark fairy's voice. "Think you can escape me?"

"Leave her alone!" Dawn said, smacking him with the dry eraser. He startled awake.

"Wh-what's happening?" he stammered, seeing all his students lurching toward them.

"Just . . . go back to sleep," Dawn said, meeting his eyes. "You'll forget everything."

On command, Mr. Blankenship fell asleep again. Maybe the curse did have perks, she thought darkly. But the kids were still coming for them.

They shuffled with their arms outstretched. They moved slowly but with great determination.

"Come on, quick!" Dawn grabbed Phillipa's hand, and they ran for the door, then slammed it behind them. Dawn dragged a chair to the door and wedged it under the doorknob.

Suddenly—

Bang!

Leah smacked the window in the door, then pushed her face into it. "Give it back! The spinning wheel belongs to me! How dare you try to deceive the Mistress of All Evil?"

She was speaking in Maleficent's voice.

The door rattled as Leah bashed her body into it over and over, but it held fast. Dawn and Phillipa didn't have any time to lose. The chair would only hold it for so long.

Together they bolted down the hall and ran for their bikes.

They rode away from the school as fast as they could, only pausing to rest on the outskirts of town, down by the woods.

Dawn's heart was still racing. "Wow, that was close! So much for school."

"That was freaky," Phillipa said. But fortunately, she looked wide-awake.

"Maleficent is bewitching people," Dawn said. "Anyone I look at . . ."

"She possesses them," Phillipa agreed. "Makes them do her bidding."

"Exactly," Dawn said. "What are we going to do? The buyer is coming today."

Phillipa thought it over. "Well, I have a plan. It's a long shot. But it's the best I've got."

"What is it?" Dawn said, feeling hope stir in her heart.

"When the buyer shows up to collect the spinning wheel today," Phillipa said, "your aunts will have to unlock the safe, right? Well, maybe we can sneak off with the spinning wheel and destroy it. That way, we can end the sleeping curse once and for all."

"Wow, that's brilliant," Dawn said, exuding optimism for the first time.

"Thanks," Phillipa said, blushing.

Phillipa pointed to her backpack. "I brought supplies for our mission." She unzipped it. Dawn saw inside crumpled newspaper and a lighter.

"What's that for?" Dawn asked, pulling the lighter out and flicking it. It burst into flame.

"Once we get the spinning wheel from your aunts, we'll burn it in a bonfire," Phillipa said with a serious expression. "That's the only way to defeat the dark fairy. If her power is infused in the wheel, then it should weaken her . . . permanently."

"Okay, let's wait a little bit until after school hours," Dawn said. "Then we can head over to the antique shop."

"I just hope it works," Phillipa said. "I mean, I've read books about stuff like this. But those are made-up stories. It's much scarier when it's real life. My books always have happy endings. I hope that's how our story turns out, too."

Dawn gave her a worried look. "Maleficent won't be easily deceived—"

Caw! Caw!

Suddenly, ravens swarmed overhead, almost like the dark fairy was spying on them. Dawn cowered. She had a bad feeling about it.

But this was their only hope. They had to try.

18
BONFIRE OF THE
SPINNING WHEELS

*J*ingle.

Dawn entered the shop, hearing her aunts' cheerful voices coming from behind the register. "The buyer should be here any minute to collect the spinning wheel," Aunt Merry chirped to Fleur in excitement.

"Did you fetch it from the safe yet?" Aunt Fleur said, rushing around. "We should polish it up, make sure it's in tip-top shape!"

Dawn waited while Merry headed into the back office, then brought the spinning wheel out and placed it on the counter.

She was bent over, pulling out the wood polish, when Dawn hurried toward them.

BONFIRE OF THE SPINNING WHEELS

"Uh, let me help!" she said in a cheerful voice, bustling into the shop as if she'd arrived that moment to begin work. She made sure to look them both in the eye. "I can polish it up for you."

And just like that, both of her aunts fell asleep on their feet, snoring away that instant.

Dawn quickly swiped the spinning wheel off the counter. She lugged it toward the back screened door. This was the first time she'd touched it since that day in the shed, and it felt heavy in her hands. And powerful . . .

Out back, Phillipa was standing by a pile of wood she'd stacked to set up a bonfire. Newspaper was stuffed under it. She clutched the lighter, ready to set it ablaze.

"Well, what are you waiting for?" Dawn said. She felt a rush of fear. "Hurry up, light it. We don't have much time."

Phillipa flicked the lighter, causing it to spark and catch fire, then touched it to the newspaper. It went up in flames immediately, spreading from the kindling to the dry wood. Soon, it had turned into a proper fire with searing hot flames.

Dawn carried the wheel to it.

"Go ahead, toss it in!" Phillipa called.

"What're you girls doing?"

Dawn jerked around. An old woman in a green velvet hooded cloak stood at the back door. She walked with a gnarled cane and a limp. *This must be the buyer,* Dawn realized with a start.

"Is that my spinning wheel?" the old woman said, sounding upset. Her face remained shrouded by the hood, cast in shadow. But Dawn could feel her eyes on them.

"Uh, you're not allowed back here," Dawn said without hesitating, clutching the wheel tighter. She held it over the bonfire. The flames licked higher, wanting to claim it for tinder.

"The shopkeepers were sound asleep behind the register, so I wandered out back," the old woman went on. "I came today to fetch my new purchase, if you please. I bought it at the auction house. Paid a hefty price, too."

"No, I'm so sorry," Dawn said. "But I can't give it you. You won't believe me, but this wheel contains dark magic. It's too dangerous. We have to destroy it—"

The old lady threw back her hood. Her eyes flashed with yellow light.

"Give me the wheel!" the women whispered harshly. "Or I'll destroy you!"

Her voice belonged to Maleficent.

Dawn stared at her in horror. She realized that the dark fairy must have bewitched the buyer, using her to retrieve the spinning wheel. It had to be given back willingly. So she had known that Dawn's aunts would simply hand it over to the old woman, who could then bring it to the fairy.

It was a brilliant plan—and it had almost worked, too.

The old lady lurched toward them, throwing down her cane and moving with surprising speed. The dark magic seemed to propel her unnaturally.

Dawn staggered back, falling to her knees.

She dropped the spinning wheel. The old lady lunged for it, but Samson leapt between her and the antique. He barked, baring his teeth and growling.

"Hurry, grab the wheel!" Phillipa yelled. "Throw it in the fire!"

Samson barked fiercely again. That was all Dawn needed to hear. She grabbed the spinning wheel and held it over the flames.

"No, give it back!" the old woman screeched in desperation. Samson snagged her cloak, but it tore. She lunged toward Dawn. Her hands turned into sharp claws.

"Never!" Dawn said, throwing herself between the old woman and the flames.

Then, she tossed the spinning wheel onto the bonfire. She cringed back, expecting it to burst into flames—

But the flames smoldered and smoked, dying out immediately, as if sucked into the spinning wheel.

"Oh, no," Phillipa said in horror. "It's not working. The fire went out."

"But why didn't it burn up?" Dawn asked, shocked by this turn of events.

"You poor simple fools!" the old woman screeched. "You think *my* spinning wheel can be destroyed by mortals and mere flames?"

She cackled hideously in the dark fairy's voice.

"Give it to me—or else!"

Phillipa whispered to Dawn frantically, "No matter what happens, don't give it to her! She's too dangerous."

The old lady tried to grab the wheel from the charred

woodpile, but as soon as she touched it, emerald flames shot out. Her hands caught fire.

"Noooooo!" the old woman howled.

The protection spells had been triggered.

Dawn grabbed a nearby broom and fished the wheel out of the extinguished bonfire. But surprisingly, it was cool to the touch. She clutched it to her chest, backing away from the old woman.

"Or else what?" she said. "You need me to give it back, right? You can't just take it. That's why you tried to trick my aunts. That's why it burned you when you touched it."

"You made a deal!" the old woman whispered fiercely. Her blackened hands looked like skeletal stumps. The protection spells were powerful. "It belongs to me."

"No, I won't do it," Dawn said, staring her down, "and let you hurt and curse more people! There's a reason they hid it from you. We know what you did to Princess Aurora."

"Oh, her parents deserved to be punished," the old woman said, cackling, in the dark fairy's voice. "Just like your little frenemy for not inviting you to her birthday?"

"No, that's where you're wrong," Dawn said. "I'm not letting you have it. You're evil!"

A furious expression swept over the old woman's face.

"Oh, you want to play dirty?" she said in a malevolent voice. She got a glint in her eye, glancing over at Phillipa. "Think you can outsmart me? The Mistress of All Evil!"

Before Dawn could reply, the old woman lunged, but this time at Phillipa.

She grabbed her and wheeled around. Immediately, Phillipa fell asleep in her arms, sagging forward helplessly.

"Wait, what're you doing?" Dawn asked, panicked. "Let my friend go!"

"You took something of mine," the old woman hissed in the dark fairy's voice. "So now I'm taking something that belongs to you."

"No, you can't!" Dawn screamed.

But it was too late.

"Bring me the spinning wheel before the sun sets tomorrow," the old woman said, holding Phillipa's limp body. "Or else your friend will sleep . . . forever."

19
THE TOWNS! THE FOREST! THE MOUNTAINS!

"**N**o, bring her back!"

Dawn tried to stop the woman from vanishing with Phillipa, but they were gone in a flash. The smoke she left behind dissipated until Dawn was left alone with the cursed spinning wheel.

Not only had their plan to destroy the wheel totally failed, but now her only friend here was in danger, too. She'd been cursed with the sleeping sickness and kidnapped by the dark fairy.

"Dearie, are you okay?" Aunt Merry called.

Her aunts both dashed through the door, looking confused. They saw the spinning wheel in Dawn's arms and the smoldering ruins of the bonfire. They both gasped in alarm.

"Oh, no, what did you do?" Aunt Fleur said.

"What happened to the buyer?" Aunt Merry said, scanning the back area by the shed. "She was supposed to be here already!"

Dawn felt terrible. She knew they meant the best, but she couldn't let them have the spinning wheel back. They wouldn't understand.

"I'm so sorry . . ." Dawn said, meeting their eyes for a moment and willing them to sleep.

Promptly, both aunts dozed off once again. Dawn knew they'd be okay . . . for now. However, if she didn't stop the dark fairy from getting her spinning wheel back, then everyone afflicted by the sleeping curse would die.

And she had to save Phillipa.

First, she had to get the wheel to safety. She grabbed it and strapped it to the back of her bike with some bungee cords from the shed. She also spotted something else — the antique sword.

She grabbed it, put it in the bike basket, then took off, pedaling furiously. She glanced back one last time. Her aunts were still sound asleep on their feet in the backyard, unaware of the danger that threatened them all now.

It's all my fault, Dawn thought as she rode away.

And she promised herself she was going to find a way to save her friend and fix it.

Even if it was the last thing she did.

* * *

Dawn kept pedaling as fast as she could, cutting across the fields and away from the dusty roads, where she'd be easily spotted. She had sunglasses with her just in case.

Finally, she found a deserted clearing just inside the tree line by the forest. Occasionally, she heard the roar of a car driving past, but mostly just the sweet chirping of birds and whisper of leaves being swept by a mild breeze.

She pulled over, leaned her bike against a tree, then slumped down to think. How was she going to find Phillipa and rescue her?

The bewitched woman could have taken her anywhere. They'd vanished in a puff of green smoke. The dark fairy's words, uttered from the woman's mouth, echoed through her head.

But Dawn knew she couldn't give the spinning wheel

to Maleficent, or the dark fairy could transform her sleeping curse into a death curse. Anyone affected by it could perish.

She also didn't have much time left. Her aunts would wake up soon. And they'd come looking for her, especially once they discovered the spinning wheel was gone.

What am I going to do?

Dawn sniffled, feeling a hard lump form in her throat. She felt completely hopeless and lost. More than anything, she wished she'd never gotten in trouble, never been sent away, never found that spinning wheel, and *especially* never made that deal with the dark fairy.

But like some things in life, the past could not be undone. It could only be endured and maybe, one day if you were lucky, righted by your future choices.

Caw! Caw!

The ravens were back.

They swarmed over Dawn's head and dove at her in anger. They had glowing yellow eyes, unnatural eyes—eyes like the dark fairy's.

One raven almost clipped her cheek. She tried to grab her bike, but the ravens drove her from it.

"No, get away from me!" she yelled, swatting at them.

But it was no use. They kept coming at her. She covered her face and ran for shelter in the thick underbrush. She hid under the branches and leaves. She could hear the ravens screaming and circling overhead.

She ducked lower, trying to hide herself from the unkindness of ravens.

Then suddenly—

Snort. Snort.

Something large stirred in the undergrowth. It made a terrifying noise as it trampled its way through the forest, snuffling at the air.

"What was that?" Dawn gasped.

It snorted again and raised its hairy head, staring right at her.

The creature was only a few short feet away from her face. It was covered in wiry brown hair. Two giant tusks protruded from its mouth, ready to maul any unsuspecting prey it came across. But something else stood out about it—

The creature had glowing *yellow* eyes.

Dawn felt her heart leap into her throat. Fear rushed through her, to the point where she tasted metal in her mouth. Her brain struggled to understand—

Oh, no, killer pigs, Dawn remembered. Phillipa had warned her about them. Now that she saw one, she realized it looked *nothing* like Wilbur from *Charlotte's Web*.

This creature was a monster.

The pig locked on to her, hypnotizing her with its unnatural eyes. Dawn froze, caught in its bewitched gaze. The feral pig roared, baring its sharp teeth as its tusks stabbed the air.

That snapped Dawn out of her trance.

She scrambled away, backing up as fast as she could, but a branch caught her foot. Dawn tripped, falling flat on her back. She pried herself up, feeling pain tear through her. Then she tried to scramble back to her bike and the spinning wheel.

But more yellow eyes popped open around her.

Dawn gasped again. There was a whole pack of feral pigs. They snorted, pawed, and huffed at the air.

And they seemingly wanted one thing: to grab her by their strong jaws and rip her to shreds.

"No, leave me alone!" Dawn cried.

She ran through the forest as fast as she could, even as one of the feral pigs slashed her. She could hear the hogs coming, trampling the underbrush with their cloven hooves. It sounded like a stampede.

They moved fast.

Like something was spurring them onward. Something unnatural and fierce.

And they were gaining on her.

Dawn tried to run faster, but a branch hit her midsection, knocking the wind out of her. She struggled back to her feet, sucking down air and trying to run again.

The sun had set.

The bewitched monsters' glowing yellow eyes cut through the inky darkness. They were locked on to her. At least five feral pigs charged at her.

She knew she was done for. Dawn shut her eyes and braced herself. . . .

20
FOREST OF THORNS

Woof! Woof!

Samson burst from the woods and charged between her and the bewitched pigs. He was bigger than them — and he wasn't afraid.

"Samson!" Dawn yelled in gratitude.

The huge dog stared the feral pigs down, then chased them into the woods.

Once the creatures were gone, he returned to her side. His pink tongue lolled out of his mouth as he licked her hands, but then he whined.

Dawn knew the reason.

He misses Phillipa.

"Hey, boy, thanks for saving me," Dawn said, petting his head.

"It's so dark," she said. "Can you lead me back to my bike?"

Samson barked happily and led her through the woods. The moon had risen, granting them some light, and his coat was bright white, making it easy to follow him through the trees.

A few minutes later, they arrived at her bike, still propped up and not too far from the road, but hidden inside the edge of the forest. Fortunately, the spinning wheel and her stuff remained untouched. She breathed a sigh of relief, running her hand over the antique wheel.

"Thanks, boy," Dawn said, giving Samson another head scratch. "You're a prince. You saved me."

He whined again and buried his head into her side.

"I know you miss her. I do, too."

Dawn felt sadness growing inside her like a deep pool of water, drowning her heart in its dark, murky depths.

"It's all my fault, too," she said to Samson. "Please forgive me?"

She felt tears falling, probably sourced from that internal well of sadness. He licked at her face, and in some unspoken way, she knew that he forgave her.

But then Samson backed up and barked.

"I know . . ." Dawn started.

But then, he barked more insistently. He gently grabbed her sleeve, trying to pull her deeper into the forest.

"Hey, boy, the woods are dangerous," Dawn said. "The dark fairy might find us. Or those pigs might come back."

But Samson barked and tugged harder, trying to get her to follow him. Dawn remembered the rose garden maze and how he had saved them.

"Wait, boy, what is it?" Dawn said. "Do you know where to find Phillipa?"

He barked excitedly at the mention of her name, then started sniffing the ground. He turned back for Dawn. *Woof! Woof!*

Dawn hesitated. She'd only ever been on the outskirts of the forest, and even that was creepy enough.

Samson barked impatiently.

"You're right, boy," Dawn said, taking a deep breath

to steady her nerves. Her heart hammered anyway. "We don't have much time left. We have to save her."

She grabbed her bike, then followed Samson, as he cut a path through the forest. He led her in the opposite direction of where the killer pigs had chased her. It made sense, in a way. If they were bewitched by the dark fairy, then they wouldn't want her to find her friend.

"Lead me to Phillipa!" Dawn called.

He woofed and took off at a faster clip now. It was darker the deeper they went into the thick trees of the foreboding forest. This was pitch-black—the kind that felt thick and impenetrable.

Suddenly—

Lightning lit up the forest; then thunder crackled. The wind also picked up, shrieking through the trees, making their branches rattle around.

"Hurry, boy!" Dawn called.

Samson barked and increased his speed. Dawn pedaled harder. They needed to outpace the unnatural storm brewing around them.

Branches smacked her face and sliced her cheeks, but she ignored them.

The path Samson was tracking was pounded-down dirt, and in the quick flashes of lightning, Dawn saw fresh footprints marring the earth.

Then, right when Dawn feared that they were horribly lost or, worse, about to become a snack for some hideous creature lurking in the woods, she saw the glow of artificial light ahead.

"Look, boy!" she called to Samson.

They pushed in that direction. Dawn pedaled faster, and they emerged on the outskirts of town. She slipped on her sunglasses, which made it hard to see in the dim light.

Even though it was night, the lights were still on in all the shops, and the signs were flipped to *Open*. Yet it was quiet. Too quiet.

Dawn followed Samson, biking through the center of town. A pickup truck appeared to have crashed into a metal dumpster. The truck's radiator was smoking, with steam hissing out from under the hood. A green station wagon idled beside the town's one stop sign. It sat in a pool of light cast by the streetlamps lining the block.

Dawn biked over and peered through the window, then started back in shock.

The driver was asleep at the wheel.

He was a middle-aged man . . . and strapped into the passenger seat next to him was Fred, her classmate. He was also fast asleep; he'd been playing a video game on his phone.

The beeping of his phone and the soft hum of the car's engine made it even more terrifying.

Now that Dawn was closer, she could see pedestrians frozen on the streets, mid-conversation but now snoring away on their feet. Even though she wore her sunglasses, it didn't matter. She slipped them off. The curse had grown stronger.

Now the whole town was affected.

Woof! Samson barked, then whined, sensing that something was terribly wrong.

He trotted over and licked the face of a little boy, who was fast asleep holding his mother's hand. He couldn't have been much older than two. He held a lollipop and was in the middle of eating it. But even Samson's magic couldn't wake the child from his slumber.

Dawn's stomach churned with a potent mixture of fear and dread, a nauseating combination. The people on the sidewalks didn't wake up, not even when she shook them. They were dead asleep—and it seemed like this time, nothing could wake them up.

Maleficent had cursed all of Castletown with the sleeping sickness.

That was why the lights were on. That was why the shops weren't closed. Everyone had fallen asleep where they were standing, even if it was in the middle of driving or walking somewhere.

Dawn leaned her bike against the rack. It still had the spinning wheel and sword strapped to it. Maybe she could find someone who wasn't cursed, or who she could wake up.

She approached the drugstore she and Phillipa had visited two days earlier and peered through the front door.

Dawn pushed it open and entered the store.

Shoppers stood in the aisles, clutching baskets filled with items, yet asleep in the middle of shopping. They looked so peaceful like that.

But they were all cursed.

Dawn found the shopkeeper halfway through checking out a customer, an elderly woman with dyed red hair, clutching an oversized handbag stuffed to the brim. She held a credit card in her hand. They were both snoring loudly.

Dawn nudged Mr. Crowley, but he didn't wake up. He continued snoring. He didn't even stir.

"C'mon, Mr. Crowley!"

But he remained dead asleep. Dawn swallowed hard and backed away.

Suddenly, the shopkeeper's head snapped around—

And he lurched at her. His eyes were shut, but his lips curled back in rage.

"Poor simple fool!" he hissed in the dark fairy's voice.

Dawn ducked down, and he barely missed tackling her.

She bolted through the front door and slammed it shut, making the bell jangle gleefully. The shopkeeper fumbled at the doorknob but couldn't operate it with his shaky hands. He was stuck inside.

Dawn felt relieved and backed away slowly.

Suddenly, though . . .

He broke through the glass on the door! It shattered into pieces, cutting her face and spilling onto the sidewalk, like tiny diamonds. Blood trickled down her cheeks. She scrambled away but tripped and fell back. He stumbled toward Dawn with his arms outstretched.

His eyes were shut, but his lips moved.

"Give it back," the man hissed, "or all the powers of hell shall be unleashed upon you!"

21
ALL THE POWERS OF HELL

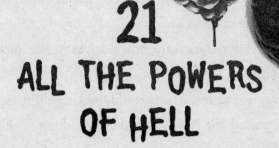

"**H**elp!" Dawn yelled. "Mr. Crowley, please wake up!"

But the shopkeeper didn't. His aim was dead-on. She dodged out of the way just in time.

His arms whiffed at thin air as Dawn remained barely out of reach.

Dawn leapt to her feet and ran for her bike, while Samson barked wildly. The shopkeeper still staggered toward her, undeterred by Samson's growls and teeth.

"Don't hurt him, boy!" Dawn called to Samson. "He doesn't know what he's doing!"

Lightning stirred overhead, then flashed over the center of town. Loud thunder exploded.

All of a sudden, as if woken by the lightning, everyone in town came to life.

They started lurching toward Dawn. She mounted her bike.

She rode as fast as she could, picking up speed. But as she passed the station wagon, still idling at the stop sign, Fred leapt out of the passenger seat. She stared at her classmate in horror.

He jumped at her, trying to tackle her off her bike—even as she was racing by.

"No, get off me!" Dawn yelled, kicking at him.

Fred absorbed the blows like they were nothing. And he wouldn't give up. He jerked his head toward the spinning wheel and grabbed for it—

But then he howled in agony, as green fire erupted from it and singed his hand. Fred fell down, writhing in pain and clutching his hand.

"Sorry, Fred," Dawn said. "You'll feel better tomorrow . . . I hope."

But Dawn had an idea now. She could use the wheel to keep the other entranced townspeople away from her.

Their feet dragged on the pavement, but they continued relentlessly.

Dawn grabbed the spinning wheel and held it up.

"Don't come any closer!" she yelled. "Or it'll zap you!"

Hands reached for the wheel, activating the protection spells. A ring of green flames exploded out of the wheel, encircling Dawn and Samson.

"That's right," Dawn yelled, grabbing her bike. "Stay back."

This time, she strapped the wheel to the front of her bike, where it could protect her. Then, she got on. She sailed out of the town center, cutting a path through the mob of townspeople, using the wheel's powers to keep them away.

She glanced back. The possessed mob of townspeople had stopped their sleepwalking and now simply stood asleep in the middle of town.

I have to fix this, she thought as she pedaled as hard as she could, *for all of them.*

Despite her heart still pounding and her increasing adrenaline, Dawn had come up with a plan. The spinning wheel the dark fairy coveted could be used to protect them from her. Dawn also had the sword that looked like the one the prince in the tapestries had used. These were now Dawn's weapons. Maybe the wheel could be used for other things, too? Could it stop the curse? And even defeat the dark fairy?

Hope blossomed in her heart for the first time in a long while. *I'm going to save my friend,* she thought, *even if it's the last thing I do.*

"Which way, boy?" Dawn called to Samson.

He barked, then led her down a familiar road. Dawn pedaled after him, recognizing the terrain. They were heading for Phillipa's house.

"Is that where the fairy took her?" Dawn asked.

Samson barked, as if to say yes.

The closer they got to the castle-like home, the more the storm overhead intensified. Wind whipped at her, trying to tear her from her seat.

But Dawn gritted her teeth, ducked her head down, and pedaled harder, riding through the wrought iron gate, then screeching to a halt in front of the castle. Rose hedges surrounded the perimeter, and vines snaked up the walls, covering the entire exterior in rose blossoms.

Dawn scanned the house, looking for any sign of life. One light was on in the highest tower—Phillipa's bedroom. Samson followed her gaze and barked wildly.

"What is it, boy?" Dawn asked, looking around warily. "Is that where she is?"

Samson barked again. *Yes, yes.*

They had started toward the castle, when, suddenly, cackling laughter bellowed out from the sky, as if coming from the storm clouds overhead. Dawn froze.

Samson barked ferociously. And then—

In a great puff of emerald smoke, a black shadow materialized in front of the castle's entrance. Its eyes glowed with bright yellow light. Its staff shimmered with a crystal orb. Two horns arched from its head. It raised its arms, its robes resembling wings.

It was Maleficent, in all her dark glory.

"Stay back and let us pass!" Dawn said, pushing forward her bike with the spinning wheel strapped to it. "We just want to find my friend. This has protection spells. They'll fight you off."

The dark fairy's voice rang out.

"Poor simple fool! That may have worked on the rabble and the townsfolk, but it won't on me. It does contain power—but I have power, too. Your friend is imprisoned in her bedroom, cursed by my sleeping spell. You can't save her. It's too late."

"Liar," Dawn said. "I don't believe you. You tricked me once."

But now she knew for sure: Phillipa was locked in her bedroom. Dawn continued forward.

Maleficent cackled, but then the spinning wheel responded, too. Emerald fire simmered, igniting the antique wood. The unnatural flames formed a ring of protection around Dawn and Samson. Dawn felt emboldened as they reached the middle of the stone bridge fronting the home.

The flames had almost reached the dark fairy.

"What . . . what are you doing?" the fairy gasped, and flinched back.

But then anger crested her face.

"I'll teach you!" she bellowed. "Think you can defeat me? The Mistress of All Evil?"

With that, she started running her long fingers over the orb on her staff, summoning her magic. It glowed brighter, igniting with simmering green fire.

"A forest of thorns shall be your tomb," the dark fairy chanted in a hypnotic voice. Lightning flashed. "Born through the skies in a pit of doom! Now go with a curse and serve me well!"

In a puff of smoke, Maleficent vanished. But then—

The storm clouds overhead swirled, growing thicker and darker. Thunder rumbled ominously, then crackled dangerously. The wind picked up into gale-force speeds.

A bolt of green lightning struck down, hitting the spire that housed Phillipa's room.

It struck again and again, hitting different spots of the castle.

Everywhere the bolts hit, rose vines with razor-sharp thorns sprung up and grew unnaturally fast, surrounding the castle's entrance and keeping Dawn and Samson from reaching it. Delicate rose blossoms sprouted from them, displaying their beauty, but it was a trap. Underneath those delicate, soft petals lay sharp thorns waiting to snag and slice them.

Samson barked fiercely at the vines. He whined and looked up at the spire, which seemed impossible to reach now.

"Can you find the way through?" Dawn asked him.

He barked and stuck his nose to the ground. Then, Samson looked back.

Bark! Bark!

Dawn abandoned her bike. She took the bungee cords and strapped the spinning wheel and sword to her back. They were heavy but protected her.

Samson somehow led her through thickening vines with razor-sharp thorns. One sliced her sleeve, cutting it open and drawing blood from her arm. They reached an extremely dense area of vines. Samson wriggled under it. He looked back, urging Dawn to follow him.

But Dawn was stuck.

She couldn't fit through the vines, especially with the spinning wheel on her back. It protected them, but she couldn't get through with it constantly getting entangled.

Dawn felt hopeless. Rain started pelting down, soaking her, while the storm rumbled and intensified. It was then she hit upon an idea.

"That's it . . . the sword!" she gasped.

She seized the bejeweled hilt, unsheathed it—*shing*—and held it up. Lightning struck the castle again, reflecting off the steely double-sided blade. As she clutched the hilt tighter, Dawn felt strength travel up the sword and into her arms like magic. She felt invincible.

She raised the weapon and chopped through the rose vines. They fell away like nothing at the mere touch of the sharp blade.

Dawn stared at the sword in awe.

It's a magic sword?

She remembered the illustrations in the old book they found in the shed, of the prince wielding the "Sword of Truth." Was this the same sword?

Heartened by that thought, Dawn sliced her way toward the castle's entrance.

A few minutes later, Dawn and Samson had made it through the vines. The arched stone entrance stood before them, ready to grant access to the castle-like house.

Now all Dawn had to do was get to the top of the tower to rescue her friend. Using the wheel would help Dawn find a way to break the sleeping curse.

Suddenly, a voice roared from the sky.

"No, it cannot be!" Maleficent screamed. Her cries cut through the wind.

"Stay away!" Dawn yelled, brandishing the Sword of Truth. She held it up to the sky.

Lightning struck in front of Dawn, releasing green smoke.

Dawn and Samson both leapt back in fear as loud thunder exploded and rattled the bridge before the home's entrance. When she peeled her eyes open, Dawn gasped at what she saw. . . .

A dark shadow rose between Dawn and Samson right by the castle's entrance. Lightning struck again, illuminating its horned head.

The shadow stared at Dawn with fury.

"Now you shall deal with me," Maleficent proclaimed, "and all the powers of hell!"

She raised her staff . . .

Then she brought it down.

Crack.

Green fire exploded from it, while black smoke

billowed out, shrouding her dark shadow. Dawn ducked back, shielding her eyes from the blazing-hot inferno.

The shadow grew taller and taller before turning into . . .

A horrifying black dragon!

The creature cracked open its jaws and shot out green flames right at Dawn.

Dawn jumped back behind the thick vines she had battled through, barely escaping. A wave of heat still struck her. Terror rushed through Dawn. She remembered the cover of Phillipa's fantasy book. This only happened in fairy tales.

The dragon roared so loudly that it shook the ground under Dawn's feet. It was as tall as the castle, maybe even a little taller. It took two steps toward her—*boom, boom*—then reared its head back and shrieked, displaying fearsome teeth.

Even Samson whined and shook terribly.

The hellish beast raised its horned head, preparing to attack again. Dawn tried to hide, ducking into the vines and crawling through the brambles, feeling them tear at her skin. She still clutched the sword, but it felt like a feeble defense against this humongous, deadly creature.

The black dragon let out another blast of fire.

It hit the vines, singeing them away and exposing her. Dawn looked up in horror. The beast was staring down at her with glowing yellow eyes.

Dawn still had the sword.

But she was trapped.

The dragon let out a terrible cackle. A familiar voice emerged: "Not so fast! Think you can escape the Mistress of All Evil?"

Then, it unleashed a torrent of emerald fire.

22
FLY SWIFT AND TRUE

Fire singed Dawn's hair, as she leapt back just in time. The flames hit the stone path, cutting a deep crater into it.

Dawn dropped the sword.

It hit the ground with a loud clang, skittering a few feet away.

Dawn scrambled to grab it, but the dragon reared back to strike again. Dawn backed up, but sharp thorns stabbed at her back.

They snagged her shirt, entrapping her.

She was pinned down, unable to escape.

"Poor simple fool!" the dragon said, cackling, in the

dark fairy's hideous voice. The dragon cracked its mouth open to shoot out a bolt of flame when suddenly . . .

Woof! Woof!

Samson burst out of the vines and snapped at the dragon's long, scaly tail. He nipped at the tip as it whipped around. The dragon roared in pain and reared back in surprise.

"How dare you, foul beast?"

The dragon wheeled around to face Samson. Samson, however, was no match for this hellish, impossibly large creature. He whined and cringed, helplessly backing down.

"No, don't hurt him!" Dawn yelled in terror.

She was afraid, but something else stirred in her heart. She felt determination to keep Samson safe. The sword was in front of her. Her eyes widened as she recalled the pages of the book she and Phillipa had read about the struggle between the prince and the dragon.

Dawn twisted hard, freeing herself from the vines.

Then she dove for the sword. Her hand encircled the engraved hilt. Power surged through the blade.

It shot up her arm.

"Sword of Truth," she chanted in a clear voice, tightening her grip on the hilt, "fly swift and sure, that evil die and good endure!"

The words from the book came out of her mouth, almost as if someone else was speaking them.

The dragon wheeled back around to face her, abandoning Samson.

The dragon roared and menacingly towered over Dawn.

But Dawn thrust her arm back courageously. Lightning flashed. The tip of the sword she was holding glinted.

The dragon prepared to unleash a barrage of deadly flames. But before they could reach her, Dawn threw the sword at the dragon, just like the prince had in the book.

The blade sailed from her hand—swift and true—arcing through the air and piercing the dragon's thick hide, striking it right through the heart.

The dragon screamed and writhed, then fell from the bridge and plunged into the moat below. Smoke hissed where it hit the water. Dawn peered over the edge.

The dragon was . . . *gone*.

Slowly, the vines melted away from the castle,

dissolving into green smoke that blew away with the wind. The sun pierced the horizon, tingeing it orange-yellow, the color of hope.

The color of a new day.

Dawn couldn't believe it: Maleficent was no more.

The dark fairy had transformed herself into the dragon, but Dawn had used the Sword of Truth to slay the foul beast and vanquish Maleficent, hopefully for good.

Dawn felt herself relax. She didn't even realize she'd been holding her breath. She released it, as her stress melted away.

Dawn grabbed the spinning wheel. She carried it toward the castle's entrance. Samson trotted over and licked her hand.

"Which way, boy?"

He led her through the front doors. They strode through the cavernous stone-floored rooms. Wood arches spanned over their heads, and the walls were lined with medieval tapestries. Dawn found Phillipa's parents fast asleep in the kitchen, halfway through eating dinner.

Samson led Dawn up the stairs that twisted up to Phillipa's bedroom at the top of the tower. Dawn was winded by the time she climbed them all. Her arms ached from carrying the spinning wheel, and she was exhausted after everything else that had happened that day.

I have to save my friend, she thought.

They entered the bedroom. Phillipa was fast asleep in her canopy bed. Her eyes were closed; she looked at peace. Her chest rose and fell in even rhythm, as her breath whispered in and out.

She was alive, fortunately.

But she was still fast asleep from the dark fairy's curse. Dawn set the spinning wheel down next to the bed. She stared down at her slumbering friend but didn't know how to wake her.

"Go ahead, do your magic," Dawn said to the wheel. "Wake her up."

But nothing happened. The wheel was just like an ordinary piece of junk. No protection magic or green flames emanated from it. She tried turning the wheel, and it spun reluctantly.

But Phillipa remained fast asleep. That was when Dawn realized the curse the dark fairy had placed on her friend was stronger than the sleeping spells on the others. Even though Maleficent had perished as the slayed dragon, her magic endured. The spell refused to break.

Even Samson looked worried.

He yapped and licked Phillipa's hand.

"Come on, wake up!" Dawn said, nudging her friend. But she didn't even stir. "I defeated her—I saved you! Please, why won't you wake up? I don't understand."

Just then, something tumbled off the bed.

It was the old leather-bound book—the one they'd taken from the shed. It landed with a thud and splayed open to a page that showed the cursed princess fast asleep in her bed.

From this slumber
She shall wake
When True Love's Kiss
The spell shall break

"But I'm just her friend," Dawn said, starting to cry and feeling hopeless. "We're just kids."

How could she break the spell?

She wasn't a prince—or even a princess, for that matter.

Dawn hugged her friend tightly. Her tears fell, landing on Phillipa's cheeks.

"You're my friend—my *true* friend."

Phillipa still didn't stir. Dawn started to feel hopeless again.

Then something else occurred to Dawn, as she wept over her slumbering friend. *Puppy kisses can heal anything,* she thought. It was at least worth a shot.

"Come here, boy!" Dawn said, patting the bed.

With a joyful bark, Samson hopped up on the bed with them. He tilted his head at her and whined. "Go ahead . . . give her some kisses," Dawn said. "You can do it, boy."

Samson followed her gaze, then scrambled over and licked Phillipa's face, smothering her in sloppy kisses.

For a long moment, nothing happened.

Dawn's heart sank, plummeting like the dragon had into the moat. Samson whined and looked depressed, too. He pawed at Dawn for help as if to say, *Please wake her up.*

"I'm sorry, boy," Dawn said. "I thought it would work, but I guess I was wrong."

But then—

Phillipa yawned and stirred. Her eyes slowly opened.

23
A NEW DAWN

"**W**hat happened?" Phillipa said, rubbing her tired eyes and looking around in confusion. She sat up in bed.

"Well, that's a long story!" Dawn said, laughing and crying at the same time. She couldn't believe her idea had worked. They'd defeated the dark fairy and broken the sleeping curse. She marveled at the magic of friendship. "At least our story ends . . ."

"Happily ever after?" Phillipa said sleepily.

"Yup, you got it," Dawn said. Her thoughts turned dark again as she remembered everything that had happened. "But it didn't always feel like it would."

"How'd you save me?" Phillipa said.

"I guess it's sort of like the heroes in your books. You think all is lost, but then something keeps you going," Dawn said.

"What's that?" Phillipa asked.

"Friendship," Dawn said simply. "That's the most powerful magic, it turns out."

Phillipa reached down and picked up the book from the floor. She flipped through it to the last page, where the princess awakened from her deep slumber to find her prince.

Phillipa's eyes widened.

"Wait . . . did you actually . . . kiss me?"

Dawn snort-laughed. She gestured to the dog curled up next to them on the bed. "It was Samson who did it. He licked you awake."

"Puppy kisses!" Phillipa said.

Samson barked happily.

He went to lick her face again but then whined and backed up. Something seemed to be disturbing him.

"What's wrong?" Dawn said in confusion. "I thought he'd be happy!"

"Oh, he's probably just tired," Phillipa said, letting out another yawn. "And hungry, too. He gets moody sometimes. Especially when I forget to feed him. It's been a whole day."

"Yeah, it's called being *hangry*."

They both laughed.

"Are you hungry, boy?" Dawn asked, patting his head. She'd grown fond of him over the course of all their wild adventures—just in the past few days. "Is that it . . . you want your dinner?"

But Samson shifted and panted in distress.

Suddenly, Dawn heard noises coming from downstairs. Phillipa's parents were waking up. And in the distance were sounds of cars driving on the roads, and even a tractor starting up to plow the fields.

The whole town was awakening.

The sleeping curse had been broken, once and for all.

"What happened to me?" Phillipa asked.

"Uh, well . . . Maleficent kidnapped you and put a sleeping curse on you," she began, "then imprisoned you here.

"Samson led me to you," Dawn continued. "The

whole town kind of went all zombified and attacked us. Oh, and I had to cut through magic vines and battle a dragon."

With each word, Phillipa's eyes grew wider.

"You're kidding! Really? A real live dragon? Like in my books?"

"Yup, just like them," Dawn said with a nod. "I had to use the sword to slay it."

"Ugh, I can't believe I slept through the whole dragon part," Phillipa said.

"Trust me, in real life," Dawn went on with a knowing smile, "they're way scarier and less fun."

She held up her arm, showing Phillipa her singed shirt.

"Right, good point," Phillipa said. "It's one thing to read about it. Another to face it."

"Tell me about it," Dawn said with a relieved grin. She was grateful to have her friend back at long last.

"Thanks for saving me," Phillipa said, "and defeating the evil fairy dragon lady."

"Of course, dummy! You're my friend," Dawn said as she rolled her eyes.

But then Phillipa's face fell. She looked worried.

"What about the spinning wheel?" Phillipa said, gesturing to the antique. Samson had gone over to lie down next to it, like he was guarding it. "As long as it's around, then the dark fairy can always come back. Her power must be fused into the wheel. Only, we can't destroy it. We tried that already."

"You're right." Dawn nodded. "So what are we going to do?"

"What if we hid it?" Phillipa said, springing to her feet. Suddenly, she didn't seem tired anymore. That was a good sign. "Locked it up somewhere safe? Where it can't be found?"

"That's brilliant!" Dawn said. "Do you have an idea?"

"This house has a cellar built deep underground, just like a real castle."

"Like a dungeon?" Dawn said. "That's kind of creepy."

"Yeah, kind of like that," Phillipa said. "Remember, my house is like really old?"

Dawn nodded. "Your ancestors built it."

"Exactly," Phillipa said. "Back in those days, before we had refrigerators, the cellar was used to keep food fresh.

But now it's pretty much empty and abandoned. It would be safe down there."

"Think that would work?" Dawn said, considering the plan. They both turned to gaze at the spinning wheel. It was turning eerily on its own.

The wheel still possessed dark power.

Phillipa was right. It wasn't safe to keep it out in the world.

"Guess it's our best shot," Dawn said, grateful her friend had thought of it. "We can't let it fall into the wrong hands."

"Or *she* could come back."

Phillipa's words hung in the air ominously.

Samson barked ferociously.

"Hey, boy, it's okay," Dawn said, patting his head. But he kept growling. "You don't have to worry anymore. She's gone, remember? I slayed the dragon."

As Dawn surveyed the room with Phillipa and Samson, she started to cheer up. Finally, something good had happened. With the curse lifted and the whole town revived, she could focus on school and helping her aunts out at the shop so she could return home at the end of the semester. She still missed her parents, of course, and Ronnie and Daniella.

With everything going on, she hadn't texted them for the last few days. But she planned to fix that as soon as they dealt with the spinning wheel.

And she had finally learned her lesson, this time for good. She planned to change her behavior and do better. She'd already experienced enough trouble to last a lifetime.

"Hurry, let's lock it up," Phillipa said, "before my parents decide to come find me."

She climbed off the bed and started rifling through her desk drawers, then produced a rusty old key. "Well, what are you waiting for? Grab the spinning wheel and let's go!"

24
PRICK HER FINGER

Dawn followed Phillipa, carrying the spinning wheel.

They left Samson in Phillipa's bedroom and shut the door. He was still acting all weird, and they didn't want him to make noise and alert Phillipa's parents to what they were doing.

"Sure he's okay?" Dawn asked, as Samson scratched at the door.

He'd saved her life . . . well . . . several times—just in the last few days. She kind of liked the giant fluff monster.

"Don't worry! I'll feed him after we take care of . . . *you know what*," Phillipa said with a roll of her eyes.

Dawn cocked her eyebrow, as he scratched the door again.

"Or he'll munch on your homework?" she joked.

"Homework?" Phillipa said with a frown. "What do you mean?"

"Uh, remember how he ate your homework?" Dawn said. "I heard you tell Mr. Blankenship about it my first day at school."

"Oh, right!" Phillipa laughed. "Ha, exactly. Guess I'm still sleepy."

Dawn gave her a weird look but shook it off. They left Samson and wound their way down the stairs, going around and around and around. Dawn started to feel dizzy from all the steps.

Finally, after what seemed like an eternity, they reached the main level of the house. Muffled voices echoed out of the kitchen, accompanied by the sharp smell of coffee brewing and the sizzle of bacon hitting a skillet.

"Shhh!" Phillipa said. "My parents are down there. . . ."

They crept to the next flight of stairs, which sank down

to the basement. The further they descended, the dizzier and more tired Dawn felt.

Her eyes drooped. . . .

But then she snapped back awake.

"Come on, hurry!" Phillipa said.

The staircase wound around into the basement like a stone maze, circling into itself. The lower they went, the darker it got. No light leaked through from upstairs. They'd descended belowground.

"Sorry . . . I don't feel so good," Dawn said, pausing to lean against the wall. The spinning wheel felt so heavy in her arms. She could barely keep her eyes open.

"We're almost there!" Phillipa said.

She tugged Dawn's arm, pulling her down the last few steps and into a claustrophobic hall that led to the cellar.

Dawn's head swam, and white stars danced in her vision.

"I . . . I don't know what's wrong with me . . ." Dawn stammered, not thinking clearly.

"Listen, the cellar's just ahead," Phillipa said. "Can't you make it? Just a little more."

Dawn tried to walk, but she stumbled as her eyes closed, and she almost dropped the wheel.

"Oh, no, be careful with that!" Phillipa said, reaching out to steady her friend. "And don't accidently prick your finger. We don't want to unleash any more dark curses."

"Uh, I'm sorry . . ." Dawn managed in a drowsy voice. Her eyes kept trying to close on her. "It's like . . . I'm just so . . . exhausted . . . all of a sudden."

"Think of everything you've been through!" Phillipa said.

"Yeah, you're right," Dawn said. She'd been up all night, battling zombies and dragons, and she hadn't slept once. The wheel felt even heavier in her arms.

"Well, I'm super well-rested," Phillipa said with a snort laugh. "Want me to carry it?"

Dawn felt relieved to have such a great friend. Doing everything alone was hard.

"Thanks, you're the best," she said sleepily. Her lips felt thick and were hard to move.

Dawn handed the wheel over to Phillipa, who readily accepted it. Then, Phillipa led Dawn into the cellar, which was dark and had a thick door with a lock, just like she'd promised.

Dawn was relieved. This was the perfect hiding place to keep the spinning wheel safe from Maleficent. Nobody would ever find it down here. That door was almost impenetrable. But then, she started to feel even more exhausted as soon as they set foot inside the cellar.

She slumped down onto the floor. "Uh, I don't know what's wrong with me. . . ."

And that was when it happened. . . .

Phillipa let out a cackle.

It echoed through the dungeon.

It was in a different voice. Suddenly, green flames enveloped Phillipa, swirling around her body, as she transformed into . . .

Maleficent!

The dark fairy cocked her head and peered at Dawn with her glowing yellow eyes.

"Oh, come now, why so melancholy?"

25
AGELESS SLEEP

"**N**o, it can't be!" Dawn said, trying to scramble away but overwhelmed by exhaustion.

The desire to sleep took hold of her like an iron blanket that wouldn't relent. It enveloped her and held her tight. Her eyelids drooped, as the dark fairy let out another cackle.

"You poor simple fool!" Maleficent hissed. "You thought you could defeat me?"

She clutched her spinning wheel, stroking it like a precious treasure. At her touch, the worn wood ignited with green flames. The wheel started turning slowly, as the magic flowed through it and back into the fairy. It was making her grow even more powerful.

"I killed you!" Dawn said. "I saw you fall into the moat . . . and vanish . . ." Her voice trailed off. Her head swam, but she fought back against the spell and struggled to stay awake.

"A mere mortal can't slay the Mistress of All Evil!" Maleficent said, cackling. "You're not even a princess."

Dawn felt fear cut through her exhaustion. Now that she thought about it, she realized she had never seen a body or any other evidence that she'd actually slain the dark fairy. The dragon had simply vanished when it fell into the moat.

That also explained why Samson had been growling and acting so strange. He was trying to warn her that it wasn't her friend—it was actually the dark fairy in disguise.

She'd enchanted herself, knowing that Dawn would try to rescue her friend and would trust her enough to willingly give her the spinning wheel, which would break the powerful protection spells.

"Haven't you learned yet?" Maleficent said in a mocking voice. "Love is the true curse."

Then, she raised her staff and brought it down with a deep crack against the stone.

Caw! Caw!

In a puff of green smoke, a raven appeared and alighted on Maleficent's staff. It cocked its head and peered at Dawn with sharp, malevolent black eyes.

Maleficent stroked the raven's head. "My pet, what shall we do with her?"

The raven cawed again.

"Yes, I agree," Maleficent said.

She raised her staff and brought it down—*crack*.

Chains shot out from the wall, and Dawn felt them wrap around her wrists, shackling her. The iron held her fast.

Maleficent thrust her wrist out, and the spinning wheel floated over to Dawn. Dawn felt her arm raise up, seemingly of its own accord, and prick her finger on the sharp spindle.

Blood dripped down, hitting the stone floor. It sizzled and evaporated.

"In this place of gloom and doom," the fairy chanted, "shall become your eternal tomb."

Dawn struggled against the chains frantically, but sleep fell over her and dimmed her vision. Through half-lidded eyes, she watched as Maleficent turned to leave, her cape swishing against the floor behind her.

"A death curse?" Dawn asked, her eyelids growing heavier.

"Oh, death is far too kind a punishment for you," Maleficent said with a cackle. "I want you to suffer for all of eternity.

"A most gratifying day," the dark fairy then cooed to her raven, fondly stroking its head. "For the first time in many eons, I shall sleep well."

The last thing Dawn remembered was Maleficent shutting the door to the cellar. As it closed, reducing the ambient light to only a sliver, Dawn heard her say one last thing.

"In ageless sleep you shall find repose . . . forever."

Then, the door clicked shut.

The bolt turned. Maleficent had chained her to the wall and locked the cellar door so nobody could ever find her and awaken her from the spell.

Dawn had one final thought before she fell into a deep, ageless sleep and blackness washed over her vision for the very last time.

Now she was a sleeping beauty . . . forever. . . .

THE END